# MEMORY LEAK

# MEMORY LEAK

## Trevor Schmidt

**Salvo Press**
Portland, Oregon

This is a work of fiction. All characters and events portrayed in this novel are fictitious and not intended to represent real people or places. All rights reserved. No part of this book may be reproduced in any manner whatsoever without written permission of the publisher.

MEMORY LEAK

Copyright © 2011 by Trevor Schmidt

**Salvo Press**
Portland, Oregon
www.salvopress.com

Library of Congress Control Number: 2010914316

ISBN: 978-1-60977-013-6

Cover iStock Photos
Main image of cracked Earth by Kadir Barcin
Butterfly by Stanislav Pobytov, Russia
Brain by Comotion Design, Denmark

Printed in the United States of America

Who is the third who walks always beside you?
When I count, there are only you and I together
But when I look up ahead the white road
There is always another one walking beside you
—T.S. Eliot, from *The Wasteland*

# 1

Jonathan Hart fiddled with the knobs of his control panel and the holographic emitters instantly jumped to life. The stern man standing in front of him was bathed in light and the holo stage took on an eerie red glow. Holo cameras recorded his image and speech, sending the information to every True Vision Wall Screen, every supplement dispensary's window, and, as far as Jonathan knew, every street corner in America or perhaps the world. Jonathan was usually too busy with the controls to pay attention to what the man with salt and pepper hair said each day. He didn't have to listen. That wasn't his job. Besides, after four years of working at the government's Holo Station, Jonathan Hart knew exactly what the Supreme Leader said every day of every week of every month and so on.

The man giving his daily address was the symmetrical Commander in Chief of the United States, Liam Mail. At the end of his address, the leader spoke the motto of his administration and of the Department of Symmetry itself:

"Live not on evil."

Whatever that meant.

The holo-emitters faded out and Liam Mail was left standing amid the faint crimson glow of the Holo Stage, fidgeting with his expensive suit, concerned over the amount of lint that had found its way onto the blackest of his black outfits. Jonathan raised the lights just in time to witness a sea of Police Units clad in helmets with dark visors and full riot gear surround and usher Liam Mail to the exit. He turned to the technician beside him, a scrawny, symmetrical man with a perfect five o'clock shadow and thick glasses without a single smudge or fingerprint to be seen.

"Good job today," Jonathan said to his coworker in the same tone he used on every other day.

"Good job?" the wiry man said incredulously. "Did you see Mr. Mail at the end of the show? He looked right at me. At me!"

"I'm sure it didn't mean anything, Robert." The scrawny man cringed, "How many times do I have to tell you to call me Bob?"

Jonathan had, in fact, remembered. But, it was far more entertaining to push his buttons. Bob was a spook of a man, constantly getting himself into trouble with conspiracy theories and putting his foot in his mouth.

Bob continued in a hurried voice, more shaky than before, "Everyone knows not to look him in the eyes. Have you ever heard of someone who's looked into his eyes? No. Because they're all dead!"

"I bet some are carted off to the factories," Jonathan said, feigning empathy.

"That's reassuring," Bob said sardonically. "Could you imagine not having Reshape? We'd lose our symmetry. They might as well just kill me. I'd be better off dead than

## MEMORY LEAK

asymmetrical."

Jonathan pushed his roller chair away from the console and stood up, considering the hyperventilating man before him. He pitied Bob. The government had not yet found a spousal match for him, which was discouraging for a man over the age of thirty. Jonathan tried to recall if there was any way to speed up the process, but he hadn't heard of anyone gaming the system in that way.

"I'd better get home," Jonathan said while putting on his jacket, avoiding Bob's gaze. "Don't stay up too late thinking about it, okay?"

"Easy for you to say," Bob muttered and began nibbling at his thumbnail.

"Bob, that's bad for your symmetry."

"What isn't these days?"

Jonathan gave a mental shrug and made for one of the half-hexagon glass elevators that ran along the side of the Holo Station.

Jonathan pushed past the Holo Station's glass doors into the brisk Nattan fall. He blew hot air into his hands and walked swiftly to the subway station a few blocks to the south. As he descended the damp stairs he saw a new poster on the wall. A beautiful symmetrical woman was blowing a kiss at him; the text read "Live Not On Evil."

The glass that housed this new government artwork reflected Jonathan's image back at him. For a moment he was caught in his own gaze, unable to break free of the faultless person in the glass. The man looking back at him had a strong jaw with two-days worth of facial hair, carefully trimmed under high magnification to look as symmetrical as possible. His dark brown eyes were like a deer's, barely aware and remarkably innocent. He poked his pale white cheek twice, wondering if the fluorescent lighting made his skin look whiter than normal. He examined his nose, a nose like every other nose. It was not large or ill-shaped or too curved, it was just a plain old nose, albeit a symmetrical nose. Jonathan liked his face; even enjoyed looking at it in a mirror or occasionally through the reflection given by a pane of glass. Something on this day was amiss. Dreadfully wrong.

His mouth contorted into a frown—a face he was not used to seeing. His eyes turned to a virtually imperceptible scar between his mouth and nose. Jonathan remembered the surgeon who did his latest Reshape treatment; he had done a hack job. Anyone with eyes would know, after a short inspection, that he hadn't been thoroughly fixed yet. What if he passed a checkpoint on the way home? He made a mental note to call the treatment center as soon as he could. Mistakes like that didn't go unnoticed for long.

He ran his fingers across his short brown hair—he enjoyed the feel of short hair just after it was cut—and continued through the subway station to his line. He only had to wait a few seconds before the subway car zipped past him, coming to a smooth halt moments later. He enjoyed sitting in the silver tube and traveling at high speed, watching station after station pass him by. There was comfort in his daily rides on the rails. The sounds of the subway car gliding through endless tunnels made him feel significant and a part of something bigger than himself. It helped that the train only traveled along one path. No decisions to be made. No mistakes to be made.

He found one of the few open seats and closed his eyes

# MEMORY LEAK

**5**

gently, retreating into the depths of his subconscious in an attempt to find a happy place. He could not. All he could think about was the one millimeter white mark between his mouth and nose—a reminder of a much larger gash he had received playing hover ball a few days earlier. He doubted he would ever play that game again. Sports were dangerous for symmetry.

His dark gray Government Apartment Complex, known by its moniker GAC-114, stood amongst several identical buildings built after the housing crisis of 2047. Many people faced foreclosures during that time and the government stepped in, building multiple high-rises, each housing several hundred families. Although Jonathan was grateful for many things his government did for him, he was especially appreciative of his apartment. It was approximately 450 square feet of the most prime real estate in the country. Jonathan only shared a bathroom with eight of his neighbors because he lived in a corner unit. He wasn't sure why he had been granted the coveted corner unit, which was usually reserved for couples with a child, but he thanked Liam Mail every day for his luck.

Every time Jonathan walked into GAC-114 he was overwhelmed with a deep feeling of gratitude. As he opened the door to unit 1018 he remembered something else for which he had the government to thank. Jonathan stepped through the doorway and saw his symmetrical fiancée lying on their bed, flipping through the latest issue of *Reshape* magazine and rubbing her splendidly-smooth chocolate legs together. He closed the door and manually turned the unit's eight locks behind him.

He gazed around the apartment. It was just as he left it.

A small kitchen area upon first entering, a Government Issue spring bed, and a mirrored wall that doubled as a True Vision Wall Screen when backlit. His one reclining chair faced the mirrored wall, which was easily his favorite place to sit. If there was nothing to watch, he could always admire himself.

Jonathan turned his attention to his perfect fiancée, lying on her stomach with her dark legs dancing in the air. For a moment he stared at her perfect Northwestern African-American skin until she turned her head and smiled with her symmetrical whiter than white teeth and dark brown eyes. *I accosted his thoughts; did she prefer to be called African-American or Black?* Jonathan had always been too frightened to ask, for fear that she would be offended and call off the government match—the only match, since the Department of Symmetry only matches once.

Regardless, Jonathan smiled brightly and said, "Hello, Elle. How was work?"

"Disastrous," she said, returning her eyes to her magazine. "We did everything we could for this man, but, it seems he's going to be asymmetrical forever."

"No," Jonathan gasped and walked over to the bed, putting his hand on the small of her back. Jonathan pitied asymmetricals. Their condition was sad and sometimes frightening to see. "Surely something can be done. What will happen to him?"

Elle looked up at Jonathan as though annoyed. "The same thing that happens to all of the other asymmetricals. They have a choice. Either they work in the factories or it's the gas chamber." Elle sighed, "I do hope he chooses to work in the factories. During Liam Mail's address

# MEMORY LEAK

tonight he was saying how we need more factory workers."

Jonathan remembered the small scar on his upper lip.

"Elle, take a look at this," he moved into the light and showed her his scar.

She gazed at his flaw critically. "I thought that was taken care of," Elle said, putting her hand to her mouth, her perfect eyes showing disgust. "I didn't notice until I got off work. What if someone saw?"

"Don't worry, I'll do the job myself this time and you'll be as good as new."

Jonathan took her hands in his affectionately. Her hands remained limp and she continued scrutinizing his face. He was lucky the government paired him with such a beautiful and successful woman. Him, a Holo-Communications Specialist, matched with a plastic surgeon! Jonathan gave thanks to his idol of Liam Mail every day, as was required by section 2 of Liam's Law. On some days he was inclined to pray twice a day. This was one of those days.

*I don't know why Jonathan bought into the whole idol business, but it made him happy, so for the time being, I was happy. There was nothing false about his feelings.*

Elle dog-eared her *Reshape* magazine and motioned for Jonathan to sit down next to her on the edge of the bed.

She wrapped her arms around Jonathan's biceps and said sweetly, "I've been meaning to talk to you about something."

"Oh? Are you looking into a new surgery? Because Liam Mail says, 'One can never look too perfect. We should all strive to surpass our own views of perfection and achieve one hundred percent symmetry.' Or something to that extent."

Elle smiled. "I suppose I will need some more surgeries soon. I don't know what it is, I'm only thirty but I'm getting bags under my eyes and look at the fat on my thighs. But you're getting me off track. I—I want to go to the Conception Clinic," she blurted out and then waited for his response with anticipation.

"The Clinic? But, we're not even married yet. There's still plenty of time for that."

"I know, but my friend Anna from work just did it and so did Eve from aerobics and they couldn't be happier. I'll be the only one of my friends without one," Elle said, beginning to pout.

Jonathan ran his fingers through his short hair with his free hand, calming his nerves. *I told him it was too soon. They were only matched six months ago.*

"Have you talked to your father about this? The man will kill me if we do this without his permission. The guy could probably squash me like a bug."

"Let me worry about him," Elle pleaded. "He *is* the head of the Department of Symmetry, so I'm sure he would get behind a trip to the clinic. The more symmetricals, the better, in his mind."

"But out of wedlock?"

"We're as good as married anyway!" Elle said, releasing Jonathan's arm. "You know as well as I do that no one gets out of a government match, and I'm not getting any younger."

Jonathan's mind reeled. He had met Elle's father only a few times but his image would always be ingrained in his memory, much like the image of the supreme leader, Liam Mail. The memory of someone he could not escape and someone he had to do his best to love.

"Let me think about it until tomorrow," Jonathan reasoned. "One day isn't too much to ask, is it?"

Elle smiled using her sweetest expression. "Of course, honey."

She laid herself back down on their bed and opened her dog-eared issue of *Reshape* magazine, once again unaware of anything going on around her, acting as though she were the sole occupant of Unit 1018.

Jonathan stood up and took a few steps toward the door—into the area they used as a kitchen—and rummaged through their only cupboard for something to eat. The cupboard's sole occupant was a smashed package of GS-3. Government supplement-3, or as he called it, Government slop-three, was his least favorite of the government supplied food rations. Compound three was a milky white substance akin to oatmeal but with a metallic taste and an odor that was unbearable to his and everyone else's olfactory glands. In fact, it was what most people fed their pets, supposing they were lucky enough to have their name picked from the lottery so they could have one. Unfortunately for Jonathan, pets were usually reserved for families of three or more. *I reminded him that Liam Mail said something once about 'the greatest good for the greatest number of people;' or, was it 'the end justifies the means?' No, the latter didn't fit in this situation.*

"I'm going out," Jonathan said blithely. "Seems we let the food run out again."

Elle didn't look up from her magazine, but said, "Would you pick up those supplements I like? You know the one."

"GS-8?"

"That's it. I'm afraid I've lost my taste for one through seven."

"I'll try to find some, but you know how it is, every time they come up with a new supplement they're gone practically before they hit the shelves."

He checked his wallet for ration cards and unlocked the eight unit locks, stepping into the brisk gray hallway. Jonathan closed the door behind him. As the door shut, his neighbor's door opened and a middle-aged man stepped into the hall. The last time Jonathan had seen Evan Nave he had been balding. Since then he had shaved his head completely. The bald man now stood between Jonathan and the elevators.

"I see you're as symmetrical as ever, Mr. Nave."

*I was appalled that Jonathan gave the nosy neighbor the kindest greeting in his inventory.*

"My wife kept screaming 'embrace the bald, Evan, embrace the bald,'" Evan said imitating his wife's voice. "Finally, I just did it." He began tapping his chin, then continued, "I think I—yes, I quite like it."

"It's very becoming, Mr. Nave," Jonathan said, trying his best to avoid the aggravating man and continue to the elevators.

"Oh thank you, thank you. Now, what's this I hear about you having a baby?" Evan Nave asked Jonathan probingly.

Jonathan cringed. He had forgotten how thin his apartment's walls were. It didn't help matters to live next to the apartment complex's gossip king.

"Well, as I'm sure you heard, Mr. Nave, it isn't for sure yet and we'll be deciding shortly. Please don't tell anyone though, we'd rather keep it quiet until we know for sure."

Jonathan knew, of course, that no such promise would hold any weight coming from Mr. Nave.

"Right you are, Mr. Hart, right you are. I wouldn't dream of telling a soul. These lips are sealed," he made the motion of a key turning to lock his mouth shut. "Not a word will escape me. You have my unrelenting support in this matter."

"Thanks," Jonathan said skeptically. "Anyway, I better get to the store."

"If you want GS-8 you'll have to be quick. You best go to the corner store a few blocks down instead of the main grocery supply. Those supplements are going fast, fast, fast!"

He heard them discuss GS-8 too? Jonathan thought. What was he doing, holding his ear to the wall the entire time?

"Right, will do," he said with a nod. He walked briskly down the hall, praying to Liam Mail that no other nosy residents of GAC-114 would stop him on his way.

# 2

Jonathan stood in GAC-114's mirrored elevator watching the numbers on the wall display count down from 10 to G, listening absently to the droning elevator music. As the doors opened, Jonathan's image was split in two, revealing the complex's simple lobby. He crossed the shabby gray room and opened the glass front door, breathing in a breath of the cold city air and gazing at the gray haze beyond the Government Apartment Complexes. He coughed hard. Jonathan figured he had something caught in his throat.

"That smog will get you every time," a voice rasped from Jonathan's left.

Jonathan swung around and saw a decrepit man propped up against GAC-114's dreary brick wall. Upon closer inspection, he realized that the man was asymmetrical. Disgusting, he thought. Even if it was after dark, what was he doing in this part of town?

"Explain yourself," Jonathan said, his face contorting with revulsion. "Give me one good reason I shouldn't call the Night Watch."

The man pulled back the sleeve on his ripped brown

# MEMORY LEAK

overcoat, revealing a numerical tattoo. Next to the number was a small symbol. A black hammer. He was a factory worker.

"I can't go back there. I'll take my sentence."

Sirens blared and within seconds a police vehicle skidded to a halt mere feet from Jonathan and the asymmetrical man. Jonathan peered across the street and saw a young couple, one of whom was on their cellular phone, presumably calling in a rogue asymmetrical.

One of the Police Units pushed their car door up and stepped out onto the street. His black riot gear was barely visible against the darkening sky. The helmet's visor came down over his eyes and green words and pictures scrolled in front of what must have been his eyes. He looked from the man on the ground to Jonathan and asked robotically, "Sir, are you consorting with asymmetricals?"

"N-No sir," Jonathan stammered, always wary of Police Units. "I live in this GAC and was on my way to the store and this man accosted me."

The Night Watch Police Unit considered him for a moment, green flashes of pictures and dates and every other imaginable piece of information scrolled by on the visor, appearing backward to Jonathan.

"Move along Mr. Hart," the Police Unit said with a metallic voice emanating from his mask.

Without another word Jonathan walked swiftly down the street toward the corner store. When he reached the next street corner he looked back, much against his better judgment, and saw the asymmetrical man with a black bag over his head, being shoved in the back of the Night Watch vehicle. Moments later the vehicle sped off at a dizzying speed.

Jonathan was jealous of those who could drive motor vehicles. He understood the belief that there was no need for them in the city, but a part of him ached for the freedom a motor vehicle could provide. He remembered being inconsolable when they were made illegal before he was of legal age to drive. The streets were now for emergency vehicles only. That meant Police Units, Ambulance Units, Reshapers, and Firefighters. *I told Jonathan he shouldn't complain. He did get to ride the subway every day.* Jonathan smiled and gave thanks to Liam Mail for that luxury.

He shook off his jumbled thoughts—*thoughts were overrated in the first place*—and continued what should have been a short walk to the corner store. Inside, he rummaged through the shelves for the GS supply. He managed to find a few GS-8's and brought them to the counter. He thumbed through his wallet for his ration cards and came across one he hadn't used in months. He took it out and slid it through a small hole to the cashier behind the plate glass window.

"I'll have the ones with the red cover, please."

"Sir, these are bad for symmetry," the cashier said. "They create unsightly facial lines."

"Just give me the damn cigarettes. I'll schedule an extra treatment next week." He pushed forward the GS-8 packages. "These too."

Jonathan had only smoked a few times in his life. The ration cards usually littered his wallet until they expired, then he'd throw them away. He felt like it was a waste, but if what was said about them was true, he didn't want to risk losing his symmetry. He felt differently in that moment. Elle wanted to conceive a child. He needed some

# MEMORY LEAK 15

level of comfort, no matter how small. The red pack was the strongest, with only half of each cigarette made of the brown filter material. Even as he slid the ration card through the hole in the plate glass window he doubted if he would ever smoke a cigarette from the red pack. Everyone knew the red one was dangerous.

Regardless, a voice in his head, *my voice*, told him to take the brown paper bag stuffed with his rations. He did, grabbing a book of matches from the counter on his way out to the street corner. Run-ins with Police Units always put a damper on his mood. He took out the red package and examined the side:

*Warning: This product may be harmful to your symmetry. Those without Reshape Rations should not smoke.*

He made a smirk and put a cigarette in his mouth, shaking the book of matches just to hear the sound of the miniature wooden sticks, which was a rare pleasure. In truth, he didn't even like smoking. The taste it left on his tongue lingered long after the cigarette went out. He hated the smell of stale smoke on his clothes. *I, on the other hand, liked seeing the trail of smoke rise into the air, dissipating into nothing. Jonathan felt the urge to smoke because I was itching for a drag.*

He was never able to break free of the always-present conscious thought that Liam Mail was watching his every move. Besides, being engaged to a Reshape Surgeon, Jonathan wasn't supposed to smoke to set an example for everyone else. Elle had to follow even more stringent rules.

*I leaned on his mind for a moment.* Jonathan struck a match and watched it catch. He would have saved the match if he knew he would never get the chance to light

**16**                                                           *Trevor Schmidt*

his cigarette. The alley adjacent to the corner store erupted with a woman's screams. He let his match fall to the ground and stowed his cigarette back in its red sheath. Jonathan shuffled a few steps toward the alley and could see a young woman being confronted by two assailants. He wondered if he should call the Police Units. *Personally, I'd rather not deal with them twice in one night. I wondered if they would even get there before they injured her beyond repair. I told him to leave her; she would only bring trouble.*

A million thoughts rushed through Jonathan's brain, his neurotransmitters exhausted from the sudden call to action. *I reminded him that he shouldn't get into a fight since his symmetry was almost compromised with his scarred upper lip.*

The girl's hood slipped just enough for Jonathan to see her artificial red hair. He hadn't seen anything like it before. *Hell, I thought. He was marrying a Reshape surgeon. She should be able to fix any damage he could do to his symmetry. Couldn't she?*

Jonathan dropped his paper bag of rations and ran toward the screaming woman. As he entered the alley he searched along the sidewall for a blunt object, anything to give him an advantage. It felt as though ancient instincts were kicking in that were beyond his comprehension or control. He grabbed the first thing his hands could grasp—the lid of a metal trashcan—and smashed the first of the attackers over the back of his head. The man collapsed to his knees and then fell on his side, unconscious. He could see the gruff African-American man's face only briefly, but noticed he had graying hair and a strong jawline.

# MEMORY LEAK

Jonathan, surprised his attack had been so successful, neglected to pay attention to the second assailant, who proceeded to crush his nose in with a crowbar. He fell to the ground with a mix of pain and despair. His nose was broken and bleeding profusely. All he would remember of the attacker after that night was a flash of white, the palest man he had ever seen or would ever see again.

The girl with the red hair, now propped up against a dumpster, took this opportunity to kick out the second man's knee. When he was down she grabbed his crowbar and hit him repeatedly, occasionally making contact with ribs or his chest when he couldn't block the attacks with his hands. The man stopped fighting back and slipped into the fetal position. Jonathan wasn't sure what had happened. The girl's blows, although great in number, didn't seem strong enough to bring the man down. Almost as though she were holding back for fear of causing him serious injury. *I told him that notion was ridiculous.*

The redhead bent down over Jonathan, whose vision had gone blurry with tears of anguish. His perfect nose was a mess of cracked cartilage and chipped bone. He wondered if Elle would ever be able to fix it. Maybe he would end up at a factory. Maybe he would have a number and a hammer tattooed in his forearm. *I told him I'd rather die than work at one of the factories.* Jonathan agreed with the feeling cropping up inside him. He needed his symmetry.

"Are you all right?" the redhead asked. "Let's get you up, I can fix you at my place. At least, I'll do the best I can."

Jonathan's words came out a garbled mess of sounds lacking any notion of coherence. All he could think about was symmetry. He never asked her if she was all right.

Seven blocks away, past the Government Apartment Complexes of midtown Nattan, past where the Night Watch relentlessly patrolled, lay Old Town. In just seven blocks, a sprawling metropolis turned into an abandoned district, a decrepit ghetto broken and crumbling from years of unrest between asymmetricals and symmetricals. The inhabitants of the district were remnants of an older generation who fought to retain the old ways, which Jonathan Hart knew nothing about.

After years of unrest, Liam Mail made a truce with the asymmetricals. If they stayed in their district, they would be left alone. If they were caught venturing outside their district, they would be sent to the factories. Of course, the old district was incapable of sustaining itself, with no source of food, clean water, or anything else, and Liam Mail knew this. Eventually, they would have to leave their district and he would get his way, without spilling any more symmetrical blood.

Near the edge of the Government Apartment Complexes, the girl with the red hair helped Jonathan into Old Town. He imagined he was sitting in a Reshape chair, ready to receive his monthly treatment. Jonathan had no idea he was in Old Town, or that asymmetricals still lived there en masse. What he did know was that the girl's artificial red hair was captivating.

"It's just through here," the girl said, tired from taking so much of Jonathan's weight on her own shoulder.

"Re-Resha-."

"What's that? Never mind, we're here."

She leaned Jonathan against a wall covered with graffi-

# MEMORY LEAK

ti while she fumbled with her keys. She then dragged him inside, lighting her way with a fluorescent key chain light, and found her way to a run-down mustard yellow couch, plopping him down on the soiled cushions. While he held his bleeding nose the redhead turned on the solitary lamp and lit several candles around the room. Jonathan, however, still couldn't see her face behind the layer of tears surrounding his faultless brown eyes.

"Let me find my medkit," she said, foraging through piles of what he perceived to be junk. "It's around here some—got it! Now sit still."

She applied a cream to his nose, which bubbled up and coagulated the blood.

"That should do it for now," she said. "Let's wash you off and see what the damage is."

Jonathan stood up and felt his blood rush to his head. He was still disoriented from loss of blood and the poor lighting in the room. The room. That dingy excuse for a living space. Jonathan realized he had no idea where he was.

"Come on," the girl said from the bathroom. "In here."

He moved his heavy legs with difficulty to the bathroom. Odd, he thought, there's no mirror in here. The redhead took off his jacket and rolled up his shirtsleeves. There was no running water. Instead, the sink was full of what looked to be stale water, tinged with brown and stagnant from non-use.

"Don't think about it, just wash off your hands and then take this," she said, handing him a ratty washcloth.

"How do you live like this? Is this water clean?"

"Don't be a baby, here—" she squirted a bit of antiseptic ointment into the water and stirred it with her finger. "All better."

Reluctantly, Jonathan scrubbed his hands and wiped as much blood as he could from around his nose. He found ordinary actions difficult without the use of a mirror. How could he tell if he wiped away all of the blood? How would he be able to assess his physical appearance at all for that matter? The questions bubbled up inside him. *I told him to calm down before he made us look bad.*

"Did I get it all?" Jonathan asked into the half-light.

"Good enough for me," she replied.

Jonathan wasn't satisfied, but what could he do? He was at her mercy. She brushed a bit of red hair out of her face, a face obscured by shadows. Jonathan felt his way back out to the living room and the horrid yellow couch, which was now stained with his blood. He slumped down into the couch, which was more comfortable than he first gave it credit.

"Come into the light," Jonathan instructed.

"Why? I'd really rather—"

Jonathan took a candle from the coffee table and brought it within an inch of her face. His jaw dropped. His mind was a mess of conflicting thoughts. He could tell that at some point in the past, she might have been symmetrical. That time had long come and gone. He guessed she was in her late teens, she was thin and covered in an equally thin layer of dirt or soot or something dark and undesirable. Her clothes were a tangle of various spaghetti straps, tight fitting dark jeans, and more bracelets than Jonathan could count. *His math skills were sub-par, but the girl did have a penchant for accessories.* Her artificial red hair, dark red in the current lighting, was a stark contrast to her bright purple and white top. She wore more eyeliner than Liam Mail allowed, and he couldn't decide

## MEMORY LEAK

21

if he was permitted to like it.

"You—you're hideous! Eyes off-center, eyebrows uneven, ears unparallel. You're asymmetrical!" He took the candle away from her face, unable to look into her big hazel eyes. "Why did you bring me back here? Don't you know if I'm caught with you I'll wind up in a factory or dead? Great. This is just perfect."

Jonathan could see a tear form and roll down her cheek. That pale cheek. Now that he thought about it, even her hair was asymmetrical, parted not in the center but off to one side, her long red bangs nearly covering her left eye. How could he have missed it before? Her hair. Her artificial red hair. He had never seen such a color in all of Nattan or even in nature, if you could say there was such a thing anymore.

"For your information, you're asymmetrical too," she said meekly.

She was right. Jonathan collapsed back on the yellow couch and covered his eyes with bloodstained hands. What could he do? If he went back, they would take him in to be Reshaped. But if they couldn't make him symmetrical again, they would be forced to send him away. He knew he would have to take that chance. There was no way he would stay there. With her.

"Look," she said, "it's not all bad. In Old Town you can be whoever you want to be. I can't remember the last time I looked in the mirror."

"For good rea—" Jonathan began but stopped himself, taking pity on the young woman. "Sorry, but I should leave. I need to get to Reshape. The sooner, the better."

As Jonathan stood up, the redhead put her hand on his shoulder and sat him back in the couch's divot.

"Can't you just wait one minute?" she asked frantically.
"Why?" Jonathan asked, utterly confounded.

"Well I just wanted to thank you for saving me back there, and I understand if you want to go, but, let me thank you properly."

Jonathan's mind went immediately to the gutter. *That was my fault; he was a prude, so it was my job to look after these matters.*

She walked to a bookcase, which was filled with assorted trinkets, bottles, and the occasional book, and pulled an ancient blue bottle with a single white X emblazoned on the side. Jonathan had the distinct feeling that whatever was in that bottle would prove disastrous to his symmetry. *I told him it couldn't make matters any worse. She's a cute girl for an asymmetrical; he's got to learn to make exceptions to Liam's Laws sometimes.*

"My dad used to make this stuff, before the armistice. He called it moonshine. I've always liked the name. I hardly remember it, but my father said you could actually see the moon in the night sky. Now you just see that faint glow behind the smog."

She poured a small amount into two glasses and handed one to Jonathan.

"Drink with me and we'll call it even," she said.

Jonathan had never tasted alcohol before. Liam Mail said that alcohol could make you do things you don't want to do and worst of all, can promote asymmetry. *Maybe I was getting through to him, because he downed his glass in one gulp.*

Immediately he could feel a fast fire burning down his throat and into the pit of his stomach. He felt a sting in his veins like he was at once truly alive and also in the

# MEMORY LEAK

process of dying. It was too much for him. He hadn't ever felt anything so potent. Perhaps it was the loss of blood, *that's what he'd tell himself later*, but his eyes began to droop and he felt the overwhelming urge to curl up in a ball on the dilapidated yellow couch. He turned on his side and saw the redhead kneel next to him, smiling. She said something muffled in his ear.

"Never thought you'd be such a lightweight. By the way, the name's Alice."

# 3

A sudden burst of serotonin pulsed through his brain and woke Jonathan Hart with a jolt. He was disoriented. Gray light seeped into the small apartment through ripped curtains. He pulled back the cheap navy blue fabric and was bathed in bright light, despite the filthiness of the glass pane. Where was he? And why did his head feel like it had been smashed to bits?

A small redheaded girl—Jonathan guessed she was about sixteen—sat staring at him with her chin cupped by her dirty hands. Had she been watching him sleep? She's asymmetrical! Jonathan pushed himself a few more inches away from the girl. Every bit of distance helped put him at ease. *I'll never understand that prude of a man.*

"Who are you?" Jonathan asked. "Where am I?"

"Don't you remember anything? I've never seen anyone pass out so fast from moonshine. You're lucky you were already sitting down."

"Moonshine?" Jonathan asked, and then vaguely remembered downing the fiery substance in the blue bottle. "What was in that? Why does my head hurt?"

"You have a hangover dummy," she said and smiled.

# MEMORY LEAK

"My dad's moonshine absorbs into the bloodstream before it can even reach the stomach. It's something in the way it was made, but I'm no expert."

Jonathan's head began pounding harder as he tried to remember everything that had happened. He remembered the corner store, the alley, and finally being led back to the girl's apartment.

"Why did you bring me here?" Jonathan fumed. "Why let me fall asleep? If they find me I'm going to the factories!"

The redhead looked surprised and sat up, brushing her asymmetrical hair out of her hazel eyes.

Alice said scornfully, "Thanks for treating my wounds, Alice. Thanks for putting me up for the night. No, a thank you is beyond you symmetricals."

Jonathan opened his mouth to make a retort but thought better of it. He took a deep breath and, avoiding her gaze, said, "You look pretty young to be here all by yourself. Do you live with anyone else?"

"I'm nineteen," she said, slumping her shoulders and sulking. "Everyone thinks I'm younger, though. I've been here alone since my dad died. And my mom was killed in a raid when I was eight "

"Sorry," Jonathan said pityingly. It wasn't like him to worry about the affairs of asymmetricals. Reshape could probably help this girl. Her face looked fixable. From far away, he might not have realized her condition. "I'm sorry, but what was your name again?"

"Alice. You were half passed out by the time I introduced myself. How about you?"

"Jonathan Hart."

Alice bit her lip awkwardly, as though unsure of what to

say next.

"Look, I'm sorry I brought you here, I don't know what I was thinking," Alice finally said, standing herself up and stretching. "You symmetricals can't be seen with one of my lot. I know how it is. So go on, then. You have GPS right? Shouldn't need directions."

Jonathan considered her for a moment. Was she being serious? He decided it was best that he go before someone found out he had been in Old Town. Elle. What would she think? Had she called the Police Units?

Alice stood holding her front door ajar. Jonathan passed by her without looking her in the eyes and, when he crossed the threshold, turned to say goodbye, but the large metal door had already closed in his face. Women, he thought, inhaling a vague scent of flowers, which dispersed into the sulfuric smell of Old Town.

He took out his cellular and opened the map function. Without thinking, he placed a marker on the map indicting Alice's apartment, then began his trek back to civilization.

Jonathan kept his coat covering most of his face as he entered GAC-114. Fortunately, no one was in the lobby at that hour of the morning. He pressed the silver button to call the elevator and watched as the display quickly counted down. The doors slid open and Jonathan turned his gaze from the wall display to the open elevator. Oh no, he thought.

"Hey there, neighbor," the bald and sprightly Evan Nave said. "Thought I'd make an early appearance at work. You know how that is I'm sure. Just trying to make a positive impression on my bos—hey, what happened to

# MEMORY LEAK

27

your nose there? You better call Reshape before you go anywhere else. Reshape will fix you. They fix everyone. As I was saying I've got to make a good impression with my boss at the dispensary. I know it's no Holo Station but I like it. Not like I have a choice in the matter, anyway. Oh God, I didn't just say that, did I? Can I borrow your Liam Mail idol? I think I left mine in my work locker. Hoo-boy, not good. We can keep this between us, can't we? We're old friends. Right?"

Jonathan pushed past the fast-talking man and punched the number ten button, watching Evan Nave fade from view, still spewing idle banter, while Jonathan's dual mirrored images reformed into one. He looked awful. Luckily, his brown hair was short enough that it took quite a bit to lose its symmetry. Short haircuts were quite common in Nattan.

He had never seen his reflection look so disheveled. His nose was crusted with blood and a white synthetic polymer, which held the pieces of his nose together for the time being. His hands were crusted with blood and dark red clots hung deep under his fingernails.

Jonathan was too focused on his image in the mirrored elevator and neglected to notice the music radiating from the symmetrical holes in the wall display. It was a music that was at once pleasant and unbearably dull. Dull, because it was the same song that was always playing in every Nattan elevator Jonathan had ever ridden. To call it music was generous. Liam Mail described it as 'Calming Tones of Symmetry.' When he heard the tones he felt silent and uncontrollable urges to smash the wall display. *Those feelings were mine. Jonathan actually thought the tones helped pacify him after a long day, like waves on a white sand beach. Jonathan was a sheep. Most people were sheep.*

The elevator came to a smooth halt and he quickly made his way down the hall, doing his best to make as little noise as possible. Jonathan tested the door handle but the door was locked. He knocked on unit 1018 and heard a muffled and unattractive groan on the other side. Multiple locks clicked back and Elle opened the door. She was still symmetrical even in the morning. Grunting, she gave him a disappointed look and retreated into the small apartment. He entered silently like a sheep following a shepard.

"I can explain—"

"I can't wait; maybe you can start by explaining why you didn't call!" Elle shrieked, then realizing others could probably hear them, continued in a softer voice, "You know I almost called the Watch? That's how desperate I was."

"I was at the corner store and when I came out I was mugged. The guy hit me in the face and I passed out. I woke up this morning like this," he said, gesturing toward his asymmetrical face. *It was the best lie I could feed him given the circumstances.* "I came right home after I woke up." *I'm normally a much better liar.*

Elle stood with arms crossed, as though she were considering whether he was telling the truth. She stepped closer to Jonathan and examined his nose.

She sighed, then said matter-of-factly, "Call in to work and tell them you won't be in for the morning shows. I can fix this but it will take a few hours."

"You're the best," Jonathan beamed.

"On one condition," Elle began, and then put her hand

on Jonathan's fragile cheek, "We go to the clinic. We conceive."

Jonathan's jaw loosened and he looked at his fiancé incredulously. Was she really going to play a game with his symmetry just to conceive a child? *I told Jonathan he might not have much choice in the matter.* He lowered his gaze and said, "I'll go call my boss and tell him I'll be late."

While Jonathan called his boss, Elle sat on the armchair reading *Reshape* magazine. Or so he thought. Elle was actually thinking back over his story—it had been full of holes. Principally, how did Jonathan get synthetic polymer to close up his bleeding nose? Why did he smell so strange? That's right. She had smelled that scent once before when she was a little girl. She and her father had visited the botanical gardens in the heritage museum downtown. Flowers. Why did he smell like flowers?

Elle turned the page in her *Reshape* magazine and saw a picture of her father, Kerrek Reinier, next to her and several other Reshape surgeons. She touched the small play panel underneath the picture and the page jumped to life. Kerrek Reinier was giving a speech on the recent breakthroughs with Symmetry Science and several Reshape surgeons stood in their white lab coats behind him, as though emanating an air of trustworthiness by their presence. She pressed the button again and the picture stopped moving.

I should call my father, she thought. He's only met Jonathan a few times. If we're having a baby, he should probably know about it.

❧

"Well," Jonathan said. "They were reluctant to let me off work, but when I told them it was a symmetrical emergency they understood."

"Then we can get started," Elle said almost mechanically.

She knelt by the bed and retrieved a silver briefcase, opened it and laid it on top of the mattress. Amidst a sea of black foam sat multiple instruments, some of which Jonathan was familiar with, others he had never seen before. His beauty treatments usually consisted of pulling back skin to prevent wrinkles, application of skin moisturizers, and the occasional scar cover-up. Major reconstruction seemed to be another game entirely.

He watched as she spread a clear plastic sheet over their mattress and put on a pair of blue latex gloves. The way she spread out her equipment on the bedside table disturbed Jonathan. Mechanical, cold, he had never seen this side of her. She slipped a surgical mask over her mouth and looked to Jonathan.

"Lay down on the bed," she said, slightly muffled through her light blue mask. Jonathan obeyed and she continued, "I don't have all of the equipment I would normally have, but since we're doing this discreetly we don't have much choice. Take this pill," she said, handing him a tiny blue capsule. "It should knock you out for about three hours. Plenty of time."

He checked his watch: 0805. He didn't have to be to work until 1500 for Mr. Mail's daily address. Jonathan

## MEMORY LEAK

held the pill in his hand for a moment. He remembered Alice, the moonshine, and most recently, Evan Nave. He closed his eyes tightly. He hated taking pills, but, cringing, shoved it in his throat and swallowed. The pill took a few moments to take effect. His muscles became weak and he found that he could not move his body. His eyes remained open, watching Elle prepare her reconstructive tools. Her silky medium brown skin and her dark brown eyes the last sight he registered before his mind finally slowed and his eyelids crept shut. His last thought before fading into nothingness was that he'd rather have gulped down some moonshine.

# 4

Jonathan Hart awoke to the rumble of two subway cars passing each other. He scraped a thin layer of crust from his tear ducts. A side affect of the pill? The pill. Why wasn't he in GAC-114? He checked his watch: 1447. He was running late. How did he get on the subway car? His nose. He checked his reflection in the window opposite his seat. Flawless. He was symmetrical once again. But how had almost seven hours passed?

Only one image remained in his head from the dark hours. A cracked and crusted landscape that seemed to stretch on forever, glowing red and orange from the light of the setting sun. A purple and blue butterfly, symmetrical in the glowing light, flew around his head as though trying to tell him something. As far as Jonathan could tell, time was standing still. That image, that wasteland of fractured earth, burned itself into his mind so he would never forget its eerie glow. *I told him the image had always been burned in his head. This was just the first time he had seen it in some time. Time will tell if he believed my words.*

Jonathan frowned just to see if the image reflected in the glass was truly his and not some symmetrical doppel-

# MEMORY LEAK                                                  33

ganger. Despite the aesthetic perfection of his new nose, he felt physical pain as though it were still broken. Felt pain as though he were still asymmetrical. A mechanical voice announced his stop over the loud speaker. The subway doors opened a moment later and Jonathan stumbled out onto the platform. His legs felt like jelly. They felt like he had been walking for many days without rest. It was probably a side effect of the drug Elle gave him.

Jonathan moved quickly across the platform and up to street level. If he didn't hurry he would be late for work. Liam Mail didn't wait. The Holo Station jutted up out of the ground in front of him, a giant compared to most of the surrounding buildings. The Holo Station stood at one hundred stories, as did the Symmetry and Reshape Buildings. Their size was not a coincidence.

On Jonathan's floor he held out his ID card under a scanner, which granted him access to the studio. He made his way to the control console and input his pass code. The numbers meant nothing to him. *The numbers were his mother's birth date. In his defense, it wasn't Jonathan's fault he couldn't remember his mother's birthday, or much of anything for that matter. It was a side effect of his condition.*

Some of the other crewmembers shot Jonathan a glance, hounding him for almost being late, yet glad that he had finally made it. Jonathan was so busy setting up the sound and light console he didn't notice Bob's absence until Liam Mail began to speak.

He avoided Liam's gaze and focused on the control panel in front of him, tweaking a knob here and there so he didn't look suspicious. Where had Bob gone? This job was his life. He was babbling about how he looked in

Liam Mail's eyes. Could that have something to do with it? Could the man's ominous stare be worse than turning to mythological stone? At least Medusa's gaze left a gravestone for the dead.

Liam Mail finished his daily broadcast to the 'free world.' His image had been lifted from every True Vision Wall Screen, every dispensary window and every street corner. Mr. Mail's guards ushered him out of the room, retreating to who knows where. Jonathan was left alone, subtle crimson light emanating from the Holo Stage his only comfort.

Jonathan rolled his chair to Bob's console and checked around it for any clue where he had gone. There was nothing. He checked the few drawers underneath the console. Empty. He was out of luck.

When he tried to close the drawer it caught on something. He pulled it out a bit more and reached his hand back into the darkness. Jonathan pulled back, grasping Bob's security pass. Why would he hide that? He flipped it over. Scratched on the back were the words, "Live not on evil."

Jonathan put the pass in his pocket and made his way back to the subway station. On the car he drifted off into a half-sleep. He wasn't sure whether the sounds he heard were in his head or from the passengers around him; if what he saw was through his half-opened eyes, or in his wandering mind.

Alice's face appeared in his mind. She smiled coyly and disappeared. Why was he thinking about her? An asymmetrical. A no one. A nothing. And yet, she was all he could think or daydream about. He had saved her, and she had saved him, so they were even. He didn't owe her any-

MEMORY LEAK                                    35

thing. Then why did he want—no, why did he need to see her?

Still in a trance-like state, Jonathan absentmindedly missed his stop. He disembarked at the next station and decided to walk back. On street level he realized he was on the edge of the GACs. Old Town was a block from where he stood. There was a noticeable difference between the towers of Nattan and the crumbling ruins of Old Town. He pulled his cellular from his pocket, called up a 3D map, and walked past the last Government Apartment Complex into the heart of the asymmetrical world.

On the street outside of Alice's apartment, he saw the artificial redhead speaking with a mousy man in an overcoat three sizes too big for his body. He had several days growth of beard and a chip out of his right ear like a rat that strayed too close to a ravenous cat.

"What do you have for me?" Alice asked him.

The rat man replied, "According to the notes you found, it's the guy, it has to be."

Jonathan's phone began to buzz, and then verbally announced that the air was not safe to breathe for extended periods of time. He tried to stifle the sound but it was too late. When he looked up the rat man was gone and Alice stood with arms crossed, staring in his direction.

"You might as well come out."

Jonathan stepped out from behind a thin gray pillar.

"I'm sorry, I just—"

"You know how bad it looks? Me talking to a symmetrical?"

"What do you mean?"

"I can't be seen consorting with symmetricals any more

than you can be seen with me," Alice said, opening the door to her apartment and motioning for him to come inside.

Jonathan brushed past her and into the dimly lit apartment. He noticed that she lived on the first floor of a thin three-story house. It had been converted at one point to house multiple boarders. He sat down on the familiar mustard yellow couch—still stained with drops of his blood—and waited for Alice.

She closed the front door behind her and pointed at Jonathan. "You can't just walk back and forth between Nattan and Old Town. Are you mad?"

"I'm sorry, but…" Jonathan realized he hadn't prepared anything to say to her.

Alice bit at her fingernails and paced, as though unsure of how much to tell him. "My father was a very important man. I'm carrying out his work now that he's gone. I don't think I should say anything more right now."

"Why is that?"

"I don't know. Maybe you're a government spy. Who knows who could be listening? Maybe the Police Units are on their way here. They have spies in Old Town, did you know that?"

"Don't be ridiculous."

"Oh God," she said, visibly frightened now. "What if you've got a transmitter on you? They would know where I am. Take off your clothes. Don't give me that look, take them off now."

Alice opened her shades all the way and examined each piece of Jonathan's clothing. He didn't know exactly what she was looking for. He had only heard stories of technology like that. The government only used that kind of thing

# MEMORY LEAK 37

on asymmetricals; they would have no need to watch their own citizens. Right?

She fiddled with the extra buttons on Jonathan's shirt and pulled one off with a knife.

"Hey!" Jonathan objected.

Alice put the button in his hand and flipped it over. "Do you see?" He looked absently at the button. "Look closer." Jonathan squinted and could see a clear microchip, less than a centimeter in length. Only under high magnification could one even see the miniscule circuitry. *Jonathan wasn't one to pay attention to details. He had me for that.*

"What do we do with it?" Jonathan asked.

Alice snatched the transmitter from him and cut it open with her knife, then threw it in her sink, still full of dirty, bloody water. She looked back at Jonathan and said, "If you just dunk it in water the transmitter will still work. You have to cut open the watertight seal first. That's the only way to be sure."

They were both silent for a while. Alice averted her eyes and began fiddling with Jonathan's cellular. He watched her, unable to tear his eyes from her slender form. She wore a purple tank top and multiple bracelets on one wrist. Some looked handmade; others had strange logos on them, perhaps salvaged from a time when corporations made products to sell to the masses. She was everything he had been told he hated; yet he was captivated by her individuality. She looked up at him with her big hazel eyes. Eyes surrounded by thick black eyeliner which couldn't have been Liam-Mail-approved.

Alice cocked her head and asked, "Why did you come back?"

"I—" Jonathan searched for the right words. "I wanted to say I'm sorry. I'm sorry about how I reacted last night when I found out you're—that you're—"

"Asymmetrical," she said aloofly and went back to tinkering with the cellular.

"I was thinking about you at work. I thought about everything that happened last night. For a minute, I wished I wasn't symmetrical," Jonathan said, wondering if every one of his words was true. He hadn't actually thought about her at work. After all, he was only at work for the duration of Liam Mail's address due to his Reshape emergency. No, what Jonathan recalled was a brief second of a dream he had while riding the rails from GAC-114 to the Holo Station. Though short, the vision had been potent and the olfactory portion of his brain had run wild with the scent of flowers. His mind had actually misplaced that image and scent and the connection of the two in its internal timeline. As he would later find out, his senses of time and reality were more flawed than he knew.

Alice faced Jonathan, cocking her head to the side and showing a brief smile. Her mouth dropped for a second as she thought of what she would say, then replied, "This device has a secondary battery. When you take out the main cell, there is a hidden panel that looks like a structural part of the phone. That pops off and a secondary cell is underneath. They put them in every phone now so even if someone takes out their battery they can remotely activate the phone and track its signal."

Jonathan considered the artificial redhead incredulously. He had expected a meaningful conversation and got a technical manual for his cellular. "The government wouldn't put a feature like that in a phone," he said, on the verge of laughing.

"Wake up, Jonathan! Who do you think issued you this phone? While everyone isn't being tracked all the time, they put these features in there so they can track you if they wanted to."

"But, how do you know if they're tracking you?"

"You don't. Not usually. But I think it's pretty obvious someone wants to track you. Its probably best if you don't come here anymore."

"Alice, listen, something weird happened today and I need your help. You know all about the government and these devices. This morning I went home and my fiancée put me to sleep to fix my nose—she's a Reshape surgeon—when I woke up I was on a subway car and running late for work. When I get there, my coworker had gone missing and all I find is his nametag. Then my shirt has a transmitter in it? What's going on?"

"Do you have the tag with you?"

"Yeah, it's right here."

Alice took the tag, examined the front, and then flipped it over. The words "Live Not On Evil" remained permanently scratched in the surface.

"Live Not On Evil," she repeated.

"Liam Mail's slogan. What does that even mean? Live not on evil."

"It's a palindrome. It's spelled the same backward as it is forward. The government has been using slogans like that for years. They get people repeating the slogans and even living by them without ever really knowing what they mean."

"Do you know what it means?" Jonathan asked.

"You have to think about what Liam Mail would consider 'evil' if you want to decipher it. What I'm wondering is why your coworker would scratch those words on here."

"His name's Bob. I called him Robert a lot though; he hated that."

Alice giggled, "It's funny when parents name their kids with a symmetrical name, as though that will put them in better standing with Liam Mail."

Jonathan had never thought about symmetry in a name before. Symmetry was for shapes and faces and hands and all other parts of the body in general. Symmetry was skin deep. Or was it? He found himself questioning the concept of symmetry, but Alice interrupted his train of thought before he could reach an answer.

"On second thought, maybe you shouldn't go home. If they were tracking you they would have seen you go into Old Town. They wouldn't come in after you, but if you came back they might arrest you. Consorting with asymmetricals or some fool thing."

"I can't stay here again. Elle would kill me," Jonathan said, visibly distraught by the news that he could be wanted by the law. "Maybe I'll just take the long way back."

"Jonathan, your fiancé is probably working with the Police Units. The transmitter had to have been placed on you while you were knocked out. Under her care."

Jonathan's phone began to vibrate and a soft melody started to play. "Oh no," he said. "It's Elle."

"Don't put it on visual," Alice instructed. "Audio only."

He answered it.

"Where the hell are you?" Elle's voice demanded. Jonathan hated to talk to her when she was upset, and would rather have hung up the phone right then. *But I*

MEMORY LEAK 41

*wanted answers.*

"I was held up on my way back from work. What's the problem?"

"You were supposed to be here forty-five minutes ago. Remember? Dinner with my father?"

Damn, Jonathan thought. Wait, had he heard anything about a dinner with her father? He couldn't recall for the life of him. "I forgot, sorry."

"That's all?" she shrieked. "You're sorry? I fix up your nose and make sure you get to work on time and you can't even remember something as simple as this? Get home. Now!"

She hung up.

"Is she always like that?" Alice asked.

"Only recently. What do you think she meant, got me to work on time?"

"It's not like she could have carried you to the subway by herself."

"What if this is just a trick to get me out of Old Town? What if they take me just as I cross over into the GAC's?" Jonathan said, thinking out loud more than asking Alice her opinion.

Alice put her small, pale hand on Jonathan's shoulder affectionately. "You don't have to go. We can take apart your phone, make sure we're not being tracked, and leave. Find someplace else and stay there."

Jonathan couldn't, or wouldn't, hear her. He needed to know why his future wife was acting so strange. What had happened during those almost seven black hours? What happened under the cover of darkness? He had to find out.

"I'm going back."

"That's foolish. You said it yourself, they could be waiting for you."

"I have to know. I don't expect you to understand," Jonathan said and took her hand briefly, which was still resting upon his shoulder, squeezed, and let her hand fall by her side.

"No. I understand. Well, you'd better get it over with then. Don't let me stop you."

Jonathan took one last look at Alice and made quickly for the door. He knew if he looked back he would never leave. So, when Alice said goodbye, he merely made a wave of his hand and closed the door behind him, never turning his head. That was the last time those eyes would see Alice.

# 5

Government Apartment Complex 114 seemed empty to Jonathan, but the mind plays tricks on you when you're frightened. It can make you believe almost anything. He crossed the lobby with hasty steps until he reached the elevator. He rode the mirrored lift to the tenth floor of the $114^{th}$ tenement in the third tenement district. His footsteps reverberated down the hallway. With each step he cringed and hunched his shoulders, hoping his neighbors would not hear him coming.

Unit 1016's door opened, scaring the living daylights out of him, and a middle-aged bald man stuck his head out.

"I see you're fixed friend. I see you're back to normal. Normal? Is that what we call it? I see you're back to being symmetrical. Symmetrical is more like it. Any decisions on the conception idea? I had a feeling about you two, government match or not, you'd make some symmetrical kids."

"Evan," Jonathan stated, growing more annoyed by the second. "As much as I enjoy continually meeting you like this…I have to go."

"Nons—" Evan Nave began but was cut short by Jonathan pushing past him. "Hey," Evan called after him. "Don't you want to hear what they've been saying?"

Jonathan stopped and turned to face the aging man, now grinning a malicious smile, reveling in the chance to share juicy secrets and information not meant for any but privileged ears. He took a step toward Mr. Nave and did something that was not at all in his character. *Although it was in my character.* He grabbed Evan's shirt with both hands and with strength unknown to him brought the pitiful man within inches of his own face.

"No games, Nave," he said in a voice not his own, "tell me what was said or so help me—"

"Elle's father, he's in your apartment. He's asking questions…about you. Not the normal father-daughter discussions either. Now let go of me or I'll scream!"

"What questions?" Jonathan asked.

"He wanted to know if you got to work today. He wanted to know if the Reshape was holding. The guy was interested in everything you've been doing. But the way he talked to her was…"

He redoubled his grip and lifted the squat man off the ground.

"Like an underling rather than a daughter," Evan squeaked.

Jonathan released him and brushed invisible dust off the man's wrinkled shirt. "Whatever you hear in there, you keep it to yourself."

Evan Nave stood silently, watching Jonathan with interest as he unlocked his door. Jonathan shot Evan one last warning glance and entered his tiny apartment. An aging muscular man sat in the sole armchair with a deep scowl

## MEMORY LEAK 45

across his face. When Jonathan entered he met Kerrek's eyes only briefly, then turned to Elle in the makeshift kitchen area. He could feel the man's gaze piercing him. He had perfect symmetry despite his age, although with a few scars he might have looked like a seasoned soldier.

"I'm sorry I'm late," Jonathan managed to say.

"Save it," Elle said. "I picked up some GS-8's. Heat them up, would you?"

He did as she instructed. He knew Kerrek Reinier did not like to wait. What had he gotten himself into now?

"Elle tells me things are going well for you as head of Symmetry," Jonathan said to Kerrek.

"Does she?" Kerrek said with a deep, raspy voice. "Elle tells me you had some trouble with your symmetry recently." He stood up from the armchair and confronted Jonathan now. "Anything less than flawless isn't good enough for my daughter. Do you get me?"

"Yes, sir," Jonathan replied, remembering briefly his time in the mandatory service.

"I expect your symmetry will remain intact from now on?"

"I'll do everything in my power to retain symmetry."

Kerrek clenched his jaw, as though disgusted by Jonathan. "Looks like the supplements are done. Get to it, boy."

They ate in silence in different parts of the apartment. There was no dining table. Kerrek ate militarily, as though another soldier was waiting for him to finish so they could take his seat. He hadn't heard much about Kerrek's past. Everyone did a few years of mandatory service, but Kerrek had always struck him as a lifer. *Maybe the Symmetry Department was his cushy retirement plan, I suggested.* Jonathan couldn't stomach any more of the GS-8, even though it was the most recent and most desirable of the Government Supplements. What was started as a government program to feed the hungry turned into monitoring and dictating what citizens ate. *I never understood the government's interest in food consumption. I always thought they were supposed to defend our liberties. But who am I to think?*

Perhaps it was his future father-in-law's presence that turned his stomach in such a way. Evan Nave's words, however, still echoed in his head. His voice alone was usually enough to disturb Jonathan's stomach serenity, but this time was different. This time, he actually took Mr. Nave's words at face value.

Having finished eating, Kerrek said, "Now, Elle tells me there are a few things we need to discuss."

Jonathan couldn't finish the last of his GS-8. Rather, he nodded in agreement and looked to Elle to start the conversation.

"Well, daddy," Elle began as sweetly as possible, "Jonathan and I have been talking about the conception clinic."

Kerrek looked sick. His skin turned from white to green under the Government Issue fluorescent lights.

"You want to go with him? He's had a history of being asymmetrical. Do you want to pass that on to your kids?"

"Daddy, you know it doesn't work that way."

"Well it damned well should. Weed out the undesirables from having kids in the first place. We can screen out physical imperfections, but we can't cure stupid."

Jonathan was taken aback. "Asymmetricals aren't stupid."

# MEMORY LEAK

"What'd you say, boy?" Kerrek's face turned purple and utterly livid. "No one talks to me that way. Asymmetricals are low and stupid and repulsive and—and—"

"I met one on the street the other day, just before he was carted off, he was nice. A little hard to look at, but, I don't know, maybe they're just misunderstood."

*I told him to shut his mouth; he was opening a can of worms that he shouldn't, given Kerrek's presence.* Jonathan insisted that he had been thinking about 'the asymmetrical problem' for some time. *Doubtful, I told him. Maybe he's felt that way since he met Alice.*

"Jonathan, please," Elle said with a shaky voice.

"If you're such an asymmetrical lover, maybe I'll turn you into one myself and cart you off to the factories. A bit of manual labor would do you some good."

"Don't joke about that," Elle said. "No one ever comes back from the factories. What would I do without Jonathan?"

"I'll find a loophole, sweetheart," Kerrek said. "I'll find a way to get you matched up with a real man. One that doesn't consort with criminals."

"Just like that? You want to throw away our match because I don't despise every asymmetrical I see? You're nuts," Jonathan said, then suddenly remembering his place, "with all due respect, Mr. Reimer."

Elle slapped Jonathan hard, her ring leaving an imprint on his face.

"No one talks to my father that way. He's done more for us than you could ever understand." Jonathan opened his mouth to speak but Elle cut him off, "No, I don't want to hear it, just get out!" She stamped her foot firmly and pointed toward the door.

Jonathan hung his head and unlocked the eight apartment locks, standing with the door open for a moment. He looked back and saw Kerrek scowl, his pale face only faintly similar to Elle's. He stepped out into the hallway and turned toward Elle, about to apologize and ask for forgiveness. She took off her ring and threw it at him. It bounced off his chest and began rolling down the hall. Without another word she slammed the door in his face.

Throughout Jonathan's whole life he'd never given a damn about asymmetricals, and no one had ever said a thing to him about them, as if they were mythical beasts that didn't or shouldn't exist. He made one non-repulsive comment and his life gets turned upside down. *That's what's wrong with Nattan, I told him. It's what is wrong with both Nattan and the police state. There's never any value in contrary opinions. "Of one mind," Liam Mail used to say.*

Jonathan stared at apartment 1018 for a moment, still in shock, still wondering if he had really just blown it with a perfect, symmetrical match. He looked down the hall. A few people popped their heads out of their doors to assess the commotion. Evan Nave was not one of them. Jonathan saw the slight glint of Elle's ring against one of the floorboards and picked it up, put it in his pocket, and walked past the shameless, self-righteous onlookers.

Outside his building he looked into the dust-filled sky trying to make out one star. Any star. He could not. Jonathan took Elle's Government Issued ring from his pocket and examined it; something he had never actually done. Inscribed on the inside of the band were the words 'Live Not On Evil.' The words angered him to his core. He threw the ring as far as he could, and he watched as the

# MEMORY LEAK

golden glint arced across the street, bounced across the pavement and was swallowed by a sewer drain. *I told him not to worry, because he never needed to see that ring again.*

# 6

Sirens blared as several Police Units passed Jonathan Hart. They made no sign they were after him in particular, but he averted his face as they passed just in case. There was no telling how far Kerrek Reinier would go to prove a point. Jonathan dragged his feet as he walked in no particular direction and without a specific destination. He tried to think of a friend he could stay with, but besides Bob, who was still missing, he had only Elle. There were no hotels where he could stay. Why would there be? Everyone had a place, and if they didn't, the government would find a place for them. All of the factories had apartments attached to them so the workers never had to leave. Not that they would have anywhere to go in the first place.

Without realizing it, his feet had brought him to the edge of the Government Apartment Complexes. A government checkpoint stood less than a block in front of him. Where did that come from? He never knew where they would show up and for how long. Jonathan Hart retreated to the small crack between GAC-133 and 134, which served as an alleyway. He pushed his way past piles of black bags of putrid-smelling trash to a point about

# MEMORY LEAK

halfway down the half-lit alley, where it branched out toward Old Town. On the other side of the alley were several shacks, made haphazardly from corrugated steel, leaned up against the relatively sturdy apartment complex.

He made his way past the shacks, composed mostly of twisted metal and sleeping asymmetricals, and back to the path he knew. Alice was the last person left he could count on. And she was asymmetrical. His spine tingled. He wasn't sure if he was afraid or excited at that thought. He wasn't sure of much. *The tingle in his spine was me, causing doubt in his mind and assailing his senses as though he were waking from a nightmare in a cold sweat. Causing him pain and anguish was one of my greatest pleasures. What are friends for?*

In minutes he was rapping at her door. She answered wearing an extra large T-shirt with a picture of a tiger emblazoned on it, which fit more like a dress than a T-shirt. She leaned against the doorframe and rubbed one mismatched sock against the other.

"What are you doing here?" she asked aloofly.

"I didn't have anywhere else to go. Turns out when you defend asymmetricals, you're dead to a lot of people."

Alice smiled slightly and stepped aside. Jonathan entered the candlelit apartment.

"Give me your phone," Alice demanded.

Jonathan complied.

"If you're going to stay here, I'm taking the batteries out."

"Fair enough," Jonathan replied.

Alice dismantled his phone and placed the pieces on the coffee table. She sat down on an armchair and hugged her legs, shrinking her already tiny frame and making her seem even younger to Jonathan. He sat down on the yellow couch. It was as though it was marked as his alone after being spattered with his blood. It was the first time Jonathan Hart had ever marked his territory.

After a short interval, Alice asked, "What happened?"

"Elle, my fiancé, had her father over for dinner. He's the head of the Department of Symmetry, practically right under Liam Mail—"

"Kerrek Reinier?"

"Ye—how did you know?"

"Everyone here knows him. He's the one who turned *Reshape* from a major corporation to a government program. The Department of Symmetry Department—that's what we call it. He's the one who made it illegal to be asymmetrical. I mean—obviously it was more than just him—there were lobbyists, special interests, corrupt politicians, and all of that rot."

"I never really paid attention to those things. I guess I just did what they told me," Jonathan said, growing more depressed by the second.

Alice looked at him with pity. "So, you really stood up for asymmetricals in front of Kerrek Reinier? I heard he shot a guy once because his coffee was made the wrong way."

"Yeah."

"I heard he ripped out someone's eyes for looking at his wife."

"Yeah."

"I heard he cloned her."

"What?" Jonathan asked. "Cloned who?"

"His wife. I heard he cloned her."

Jonathan was confused. Can they actually do that?

# MEMORY LEAK 53

Apparently the only thing the asymmetricals manufactured was rumors. "I've never heard that before. That can't be right."

"It's probably just a rumor," Alice said. "Have you ever met her?"

"She died a while back—some kind of disease. Kerrek never talked about her and neither did Elle; not really."

"Oh," Alice replied meekly. "So, what happened tonight?"

"Kerrek made some comments about asymmetricals and kept suggesting I wasn't good enough for his daughter, so I defended myself and the asymmetricals," Jonathan said casually, caring less and less about the dispute as the night wore on. "Kerrek was furious; Elle, of course, agreed with her father, so I was thrown out. Elle threw her ring at me too. I guess that means it's over."

"Aren't you sad?" Alice asked genuinely.

"I'm not as upset as I thought I'd be. I've never liked Kerrek."

"What about Elle?" Alice asked with the slightest hint of jealousy.

"We were matched up by the government after college. I haven't thought about it too much, truthfully. She has a respected career and she's, well, symmetrical. What else is there?"

Alice played with a stray thread on her nearly destroyed jeans, then looked up at him with her big hazel eyes. "Do you love her?"

Jonathan was at a loss for words. He had never been asked that before. He had never asked *himself* that before. The government told him he loved every symmetrical person, but that he loved Liam Mail most of all. Until recently, he believed that.

"No," Jonathan said after a time, "I don't think so."

He wondered if that was really true. He couldn't be sure. Why would he lie?

Alice stretched her arms and legs like a cat—*Jonathan was thinking of a Siamese cat if you want to get specific*—then she got up from her armchair and made her way to the kitchen. "Something to drink?" she asked.

"Yeah, anything," Jonathan said, and then remembered his experience with moonshine. "Maybe something lighter than last time."

Alice opened two beers and brought them back to the living room, both about room temperature, and handed one to Jonathan. He had never tried beer. It was outlawed before he was of drinking age. He took a swig, swirled it in his mouth for a moment, and swallowed with difficulty. People drank this?

"It's an acquired taste," Alice said with a smile. "They really don't let you do much do they?"

"That's not true. We have the True Vision Wall Screen. There's always something to watch."

Alice looked skeptical.

"All of the stations are owned by the government now," she said. "Every show on every channel is a copy of another show with different actors and backdrops. The government only uses about ten scripts."

Jonathan knew this of course. He wasn't blind. Not really. He hadn't watched the True Vision Wall Screen in months or perhaps even years, unless it turned itself on, that is. The wall screen did that from time to time when Liam Mail really wanted you to watch something. He tried to think back and remember what he did with all of

# MEMORY LEAK

his time. He was at a loss. All he could remember was that mirrored wall, the only real feature in his apartment. And the idol of Liam Mail. But he hadn't considered giving thanks to Liam Mail since his dinner with Kerrek. *For the record, I never believed in giving thanks to Liam Mail. He spent most of his time looking in the mirror. I told him he was a ridiculous person. He didn't object.*

All Jonathan could say to her was, "Yeah." *I sighed loudly in his head.*

Alice shivered and rubbed her arms. Goosebumps formed. "I'm going to make a fire."

"Do you need—"

"I've got it," she said and smiled coyly. "I'm a big girl."

While she began building a fire in the fireplace, Jonathan took a candle and walked around her small apartment. All he had seen was the living room and the bathroom; maybe there was something else. He found another door in the half-light and tried turning the knob with no luck. It was jammed.

Alice turned around and scrambled to her feet. "No! Don't go in there."

But now Jonathan Hart was intrigued, and he pushed on the door with all his might. As he entered the room, Alice grabbed at him, trying to pull him back.

"Stop Jonathan, it's not funny!" she shrieked. "I'm not laughing here. Does it look like I'm laughing?"

He could hardly suppress his laughter. Every manner of stuffed animal lined the walls, the windowsill, the end of the bed, and he guessed the closet as well. Her room was a fairy princess room. It looked as though it had not changed since she was eight years old. Strangely, he liked it. He never had toys or dolls or anything of the sort when he was growing up. He was busy learning procedure. Learning how he should act in every given situation. He did not, however, know how to act at that particular moment.

"You think I'm weird don't you," Alice said solemnly. "You think I'm still a little girl."

Jonathan had in fact thought both of those things. But, he said, "No, not at all."

"You're not a good liar," she said and walked back to the living room defeated.

He followed her, shutting the door to her fairytale sanctuary on his way. "You're not weird," he said, sitting down on the couch. "I've just never seen a room like this before. That's a little weird, don't you think?"

Alice gave a small smile and finished lighting the fire. Instead of finding her own armchair in the firelight, she joined him on the couch. This made him a bit uncomfortable. Despite his match to Elle being called off, he felt like he would be cheating on her if he did anything this soon. Besides, she was much too young for him. He had just turned thirty-one after all. She toyed with the buttons on his shirt and looked up at him with her big eyes.

*I told his brain to stop thinking.* He brushed her dark red locks out of her eyes. *I told him to kiss her and he did, lightly at first, and then grew more and more accustomed to her soft lips and kissed her passionately.* Something he had never done with anyone. The kisses he and Elle shared were mechanical, even forced. Nothing about his kiss with Alice was strained. On the contrary, nothing had ever felt so right in his life. For a single moment he even forgot she was asymmetrical. *Jonathan always measured time in moments. Jonathan was not a very precise person.*

They did not have sex. *Jonathan Hart was a prude.* Or, maybe, he just didn't want to ruin a good thing. *I'm going with prude.* That night they slept in front of the fire in a mess of blankets and assorted throw pillows. She fell asleep in his arms and he watched her breathe in and out and in and out once again. Jonathan was fascinated by her serene expression. He felt a pull in his chest, but he didn't know what to make of it. *I let out a loud sigh, which reverberated throughout his big dumb head.*

# 7

Kerrek Reinier sat at his symmetrical oak desk in his symmetrical office in the government's Department of Symmetry. He tapped his finger on his desk with one hand and held a fine Omaramo cigar to his mouth with the other—Cuban cigars were banned for lack of a symmetrical name; Omaramos were essentially the same thing. Mr. Reinier didn't notice that the cigar itself hung at an asymmetrical angle. He pressed a button on his phone and a voice inquired, "What can I do for you Mr. Reinier?"

"Put me through to Chief Inspector Nager," he said gruffly. "Patch her through to my wall screen." He didn't like having to use Nager's subtle expertise, but he didn't have much of a choice in this case. Regan Nager was the best he had seen in all his years of service. She worked tirelessly until she found her man and asked for no recognition or reward in return. In fact, she preferred to let him take all of the glory. Private and straight-to-the-point, that was Chief Inspector Regan Nager.

"Yes, Mr. Reinier," she said then paused. "She's on line one."

Kerrek's True Vision Wall Screen polarized from a mir-

MEMORY LEAK 59

ror into a jet-black wall, a perfect one-foot by one-foot square lit up blue with a flashing image of Regan Nager. He punched the number one key on his desk's floating holographic keyboard and rose from his comfy chair. Chief Inspector Nager's image now appeared on the screen, adjusted so she was the same height as him. (That function of the True Vision Wall Screen was Liam Mail's idea). Kerrek was one of three who had the ability to make his image larger to seem more imposing to those he called. He chose not to employ that function at that time. Something told him Regan Nager wouldn't appreciate the gesture.

"Thanks Hannah, you can hang up now," he told his secretary, who had the annoying habit of listening in on his calls. Kerrek considered the stern woman on the wall screen for a moment, puffing away at his Omaramo cigar. The symmetrical woman wore a dark gray pantsuit and a stiff white blouse. Her dark brown hair was pulled back into a tight bun, and she looked like she was ready for work, despite the late hour. She pursed her lips, a clear sign that she wished for Kerrek to hurry his call along. Finally, he said, "Regan, it's been a while."

"Always a pleasure, Mr. Reinier," the calculating woman replied. "What can I do for you at this hour?"

"I need to find a missing person," he said, examining the cigar in his right hand, the golden Omaramo signature beginning to be consumed by ash. "I assure you, it is of the utmost importance or I wouldn't have called this late."

"That's all?" she asked, unable to resist intoning her frustration.

"I don't want your Night Watch screwing it up. I need this one alive. The last time they brought a guy in for reeducation he was half dead when he got here. That's why I want you to do this job yourself. I want him brought to the Department of Symmetry for questioning and, if necessary, we'll use the device."

"What's his name?"

"Jonathan Hart."

She examined her holographic screen for about twenty seconds, and then looked back to Kerrek skeptically. "I looked up his file. What's he done? His record looks clean. Wait. It says here: *engaged to Elle Reinier*. What aren't you telling me?"

Kerrek paused to take a puff from his Omaramo cigar. "He would have been my future son-in-law. He's an asymmetrical lover, though. I have reason to believe he's involved in something bigger. The sooner he's reeducated the better."

"Let me get a trace on him," she said, checking her screen for his cellular signal. She sighed and said, "You may be right. His phone has no signal. I tried activating the backup but he must have taken that out too. Only criminals know about the spare."

"I put another tracker on him this morning. It seems that one 'malfunctioned,'" he said with a hint of admiration.

Regan Nager replied, "unfortunate."

Kerrek gave a half-hearted chuckle. "If he passes a security checkpoint, uses his ration card, or gets any kind of Symmetry treatment, hell, if he takes a crap in this city I want to be the first to know the size, texture and contents. There aren't many places in Nattan left to hide."

Kerrek was referring to city toilets in all government buildings, including Government Apartment Complexes, that analyzed human excrement and urine for DNA, send-

# MEMORY LEAK

ing all information to a central database. That way, he could find a person, know if they were pregnant, carried a viral or bacterial infection, or if they were eating the proper government supplements. A useful device as far as Kerrek was concerned.

Not at all fazed by Kerrek's comments, Regan Nager replied coldly, "We'll have him by sun up. You'll be the first to know." She pressed a button on her desk and her True Vision Wall Screen polarized. Kerrek's wall screen cut to black, then slowly faded back into a mirror.

The audacity of that woman, Kerrek Reinier thought. Out of all of his pet peeves, the one that chapped him the most was when people hung up on him. It didn't happen often, and those on the other end usually found themselves in the factories. Chief Inspector Regan Nager needed to show him more respect. He made a mental note to reprimand her the next time he saw her. In all likelihood she was too valuable to send away, and her expertise too extensive to reeducate her. She had him by the balls and he knew it all too well.

He turned from the mirrored wall and walked leisurely to the window, puffing on his Omaramo cigar, which lit up bright orange in his glass reflection. Kerrek watched the city below, nearly dead, except for the occasional police unit gliding by with lights and sirens ablaze. The glass began to be pelted with droplets of rain—at least what Kerrek assumed to be rain, though the chemical makeup of the tranquil globules could hardly be considered rainwater by any scientific measurement—nevertheless it fell, as precipitation is prone to do, regardless of acidity.

# 8

During the night the fire in Alice's unit had gone out. All that remained were the blackened fragments of a large log, still flickering with flashes of red and orange beneath the burnt white bark. The image of the wasteland invaded Jonathan's head like opening his eyes in the bright sun and retaining the burning image for seconds or even minutes. The log made a popping sound, which woke Jonathan Hart in his nest of blankets and pillows. Alice was gone. Gone where? Just plain gone. Left. Departed. He was alone.

There was a note: *Had to meet a friend. Back in a while.* He thought the message was vague, but he gave a mental shrug and made his way to his feet, almost slipping on the knot of blankets. He was groggy. He couldn't remember the last time he slept on the floor. Jonathan pulled back the curtains and let in the dirty morning light. For a moment he thought the window was too grungy to see through properly, but upon rubbing and scrubbing and rubbing again at one spot, he realized the sky itself held that hue.

Jonathan Hart felt awkward in that small apartment, as though he had no business being there. He paced through the living room recounting the previous night, stopping when he reached an antique, and very out of place, bookcase. He saw the bottle of moonshine and several unlabeled bottles, none of which interested him much. On a lower shelf there was a picture of about a dozen asymmetrical men and a small girl with dirty blonde hair riding her tricycle through what would have been a serious photograph. For one brief moment Jonathan thought he recognized a few of the men, but he must have been drowsy, because he barely glanced at the photo and he didn't recognize the little girl on the tricycle.

It was then that he heard it: the smooth spinning of multiple blades cutting through the smoggy outside air. Jonathan ran to the window and looked to the sky. Beyond the newly formed dust storm, a rounded gray craft hovered in the air, black ropes dangling from it like feeble legs of a giant insect. He didn't see them repel from the craft. However, he heard them as they crashed through the door into Alice's apartment. There was nowhere to run. The Police Units had him.

There were six that he saw, dressed from head to toe in black, their visors scrolling information in backward green letters. A severe woman wearing a charcoal gray pantsuit followed closely behind. She held a small chrome laser pistol, not currently pointed at Jonathan, but intimidating nonetheless. When she made eye contact with him, he knew what kind of woman she was.

She ordered him to put his hands on his head. He complied. She ordered him to get on the ground. He complied. If there was one thing he had learned about Police Units, it was that there wasn't any point in putting up a fight. One way or another, they always won.

"What am I being charged with?" he asked her feebly.

"Keep your mouth shut," Chief Inspector Regan Nager said, attaching magnetic restraints. "Get up!"

He obeyed and was led outside where spinning dust from the Police Units' craft pelted his skin and found its way into his eyes and nostrils. The last thing he smelled was a faint odor of sulfur. He was partially blinded as he was hoisted into the vehicle. But, what he could see was a blur of brown sulfuric dust swirling in a mess of buildings. It was hardly interesting to Jonathan Hart.

What did interest him was the symmetrical woman in the pantsuit. He had never seen a Police Unit when they weren't in full riot gear. Part of him doubted whether she had ever actually worn the black garb and visor of the Police Unit grunts. *I was that part of him, naturally. But, Jonathan had a similar idea, which I credit him for having.* This woman was on another level entirely than the grunts with which Jonathan had previously associated.

Alice hid behind a teetering pillar a ways up the street, peeking around every so often to witness Jonathan's abduction. She knew there was nothing she could do. She had no weapons and she was alone. Completely alone. She watched them hoist him into the Hovering Police Craft, or HPC as it was often known, its hatch finally closed and the blades spun ever faster, shooting into the air with surprising speed.

She had no choice now. They had to assemble all of their might. But would it be enough? She slinked into the shadows of a nearby alley. It had been some time since she had visited the headquarters. She wondered if anyone would be glad to see her, or if they would accept her after her father's death.

In minutes, the HPC landed on top of the Symmetry building, atop the hundredth floor to be exact. Jonathan Hart was pushed and shoved along past a series of increasingly small rooms until they reached a bay of glass elevators. They descended down, down into the city and then below ground through a rough metallic tube, lit only with a faint blue fiber optic track. The faint tones of Liam-Mail-approved music filled Jonathan's ears. The elevator stopped at what he assumed was the deepest floor of the building. Chief Inspector Regan Nager led him and two Police Unit escorts through a white hallway to a holding chamber. She touched a pad next to a large metallic door. There was a loud clunking sound, then the door slid to the side. He was forced down into a metal chair at a metal table in a room with walls made entirely of mirrors. Four black half spheres descended from the four corners of the ceiling, recording every movement and every sound.

They left him there. An hour, two perhaps, he couldn't be sure. The Police Units must have been waiting outside the door and only Liam Mail knows what happened to the stern woman in the pantsuit. Jonathan began nodding off. He didn't sleep well the night before. With such a small amount of space between him and Alice, and because his heart had been racing at no less than one hundred beats per minute until it got tired at around three a.m. and decided to calm down. *I can attest to that since I had to hear the pitter-patter of his organic engine with only the crackling of the fire to drown out the sound.* Some time later, Jonathan heard the mirrored door click and slide open. Kerrek Reinier stepped through, his usual scowl still ingrained in his face.

# 9

Kerrek sat in the metal chair opposite Jonathan, tapping a ringed finger against the metal table, the sound chiming off the walls and reverberating in Jonathan's eardrums. *I've always found his habits annoying.* Kerrek Reinier locked eyes with him, waiting for something, though Jonathan couldn't tell what.

Finally, when the silence was overwhelming, Jonathan asked, "Why am I here?"

Kerrek continued dragging his ring across the metal table and replied, "Why are you here?"

"If I'm not being charged with anything, then I'll—"

"Then you'll what?" Kerrek's deep voice cut into him.

Jonathan was silent.

"That's what I thought," Kerrek said. "You're here because I want to talk. I want answers and you can give them to me."

"Answers?" Jonathan repeated, his voice shaking now. He added, "I don't know anything."

"How can you be so sure? I haven't even asked a question yet."

Jonathan's eyes fell to the table, and Kerrek's wandering hand, the ring on his thumb still grating against the slab of metal. The hairs on the back of his neck stood up. He couldn't stand that sound.

"I want you to tell me everything you know about VERITAS."

Jonathan let out a brief and sonorous laugh; he couldn't help himself. "Now I'm sure I don't know anything," he said cynically.

"Let's cut the shit, Hart. We have been watching you for some time now. That apartment we picked you up at, you've been there several times. It's in Old Town."

"That's all you've got? I was found in Old Town and asymmetricals live there?" Jonathan acted amused, though his insides were a tangled mess of fear. Then he said as heartily as he could, "You're going to have to do better than that!"

"What do you know about Alice?" Kerrek asked, making a smirk of his own.

"She's no one. An asymmetrical. We met by chance. That's all."

Kerrek's smirk faded. He looked up into one of the cameras and gave a little nod. The mirrored door behind him opened and a thin man in green scrubs entered with a metallic cart, packed with various devices and tools, none of which looked familiar to Jonathan Hart.

"I had hoped this would be easier, Jonathan, but you know how I hate waiting." Kerrek motioned to the man in scrubs, who Jonathan hoped was a real doctor, and said "Sodium Pentothal."

The man handed Kerrek a syringe filled with a slightly yellow-tinted liquid. Kerrek continued, "Tell me about VERITAS, or we'll have to do this the hard way."

**MEMORY LEAK** 69

He said nothing.

Kerrek sighed and called in two guards to help hold him down. Jonathan struggled against the brutish guards but soon his muscles failed him and the liquid was injected into his neck. He felt lightheaded and began to sway.

"Sodium Pentothal affects higher brain function. It takes more brainpower to lie than tell the truth. This will just help you cooperate."

Jonathan Hart had heard of Sodium Pentothal, though he could not remember from where. *It was me that told him. A person could still manage to lie, though the drug did make it difficult to shut up. All he had to do was make Kerrek believe he was telling the truth. Most of the drug's effectiveness is in making the recipient believe they could only tell the truth. Truth is a loose term by my standards.*

Kerrek waited a few minutes for the drug to take full effect. There was no clock in the room, either because Kerrek didn't want him to know the time, or because clocks are, by nature, asymmetrical. In any case, he couldn't tell how much time had passed, but he guessed it was around five to ten minutes. The drug affected his sense of time and reality. Jonathan swayed a bit, trying to retain his composure. Kerrek's face changed, he seemed almost nice, sitting there across from Jonathan in his cold, stainless steel chair.

"How are you feeling Jonathan? Can you hear me?"

Jonathan nodded and said, "Yup. Loud and clear."

"Where did you meet Alice?"

"In an alley, she was in trouble. I didn't know she was asymmetrical."

"Good. Good," Kerrek said. "What do you know about her?"

"She lives alone. She has a tiny apartment, but I like it. If I had a choice between her apartment and my apartment, I might even choose hers. The GAC's might have some modern amenities but there's character in the creaky old boards and the well-used furniture. You can light a fire in her apartment and no one will come to take you away. That's a plus. I guess she must like it too, I mean, she's not unfixable; she could have come back to Nattan. I think she likes Old Town. It's growing on me."

*Kerrek was noticeably annoyed from my perspective, but Jonathan couldn't pick up on the subtlety in the man's face in his current state of aloofness.*

"What do you know about VERITAS? Who's a part of it? Where do they meet?"

"I don't know anything about that," Jonathan replied, his head feeling heavier and heavier as the conversation went on and bobbing and swaying in time with remnants of elevator music from the ride down into the depths of Nattan.

"Do you sympathize with asymmetricals?"

"Only as much as the next guy. We should really try to fix them. They're just living over there in Old Town and I know we have the technology to make them like us. I don't understand why we don't just fix them," Jonathan lied. He knew why some people weren't fixed, even though they had the technology. Who else would work in the factories? *I gave him credit for seeing that grain of truth.*

"Do you think this is a game?" Kerrek asked, a hint of frustration in his voice.

"No. I wasn't. Would you *like* to play a game?"

Kerrek's irritation boiled over and he struck Jonathan

# MEMORY LEAK

with a closed fist. He reeled with pain, rocking back and forth in his metal chair.

"Let me tell you what I know," Kerrek said in a sinister voice. "I know that Alice is a member of VERITAS. I know that her father was once the leader of that faction. I know it was me who shot his wife and strangled him with my own hands. I watched as the light left his eyes. How does that make you feel?"

Jonathan was stunned, looking continually away from Kerrek even when he grabbed his jaw and brought his face within inches of his own.

"I asked you a question!" Kerrek screamed in Jonathan's face, dousing him with spit in the process. "To think the matchers put you with my daughter," he said derisively, giving a short laugh. "One of them and one of us, I guess."

"What did you say?"

"Don't be an idiot, Hart. They always match people of different colors together. You think it's a coincidence? In a few generations there will only be one color. Then we can marry who we want."

"The system's broken Kerrek, and you know it," Jonathan said woozily. "The symmetricals will only go along with so much before they crack and fall to pieces. The human body can only take so much."

"Don't worry your little head about it. That's my job. They'll be content when I tell them to be."

"You might as well kill me," Jonathan said, surprised at himself, but nonetheless continuing forcefully. "I'll join VERITAS. I'll put a stop to all of this. You think you can play God?"

"I AM GOD!" Kerrek screamed, once again spewing

spit at Jonathan's face.

"You're nothing. Just Liam Mail's puppet."

"I've had enough of your shit," he said. "Take him to reeducation! Don't give me that look, Hart; in a few minutes you'll be licking my boots. You'll see. A few minutes from now, we'll have never had this conversation."

Jonathan couldn't scream. Not for lack of strength or because the drug had made him weak, rather because he lacked motivation. His brain wouldn't tell him to resist. *I wouldn't tell him to resist. He was a prisoner inside himself. My prisoner. It was better that way.*

# 10

The guards dragged Jonathan's limp body to the room at the end of the hall. The door was made of sturdy steel that must have been at least six inches thick. Inside Jonathan saw a smooth metallic machine with sea foam green leather pads that formed around the body, though he was unsure of the device's purpose. It looked like a dentist's chair, though he was sure he wasn't getting his teeth cleaned. The smell of urine and bleach filled the air and he gagged and coughed and let tears well up in his eyes. Jonathan's eyelids began to droop, his tears breaching the ducts and rushing down his cheeks. Time passed in spurts. Each time he opened his eyes he was closer to the chair. Closer to that device of unknown evil.

Finally, he was lifted and positioned on the machine's green leather pads. Its huge metal frame enveloped him and several nodes attached themselves to his forehead like tiny snakes pouncing on their prey. The silver frame of the machine changed its shape to enclose Jonathan inside, as though it were made of liquid for a split second, then was made solid once again. Jonathan sat in the hollow center of the machine, the smell of bleach and urine overpowering. He was at the epicenter of the stench. The bleach must have been to clean the piss between victims. Silently, he lay wondering how many people had sat in that chair, wondering what would happen next, searching for any inkling through the sinister darkness.

Through the darkness of the machine's belly Jonathan's eyes strained; he felt a tiny pinprick in his neck. An ambiguous fluid injected itself into his veins. His eyes remained open, as though groping desperately for any sign of light. He hated the dark.

"Comfortable?" a muffled voice asked Jonathan.

He didn't reply. Not for lack of trying, rather because the fluid coursing through his veins prevented him from moving or speaking. His eyes remained wide open, unable even to blink. Jonathan's eyes were already beginning to water.

"I see the drug has taken effect," Kerrek said, waiting for Jonathan to reply. When he didn't reply, Kerrek said, "This is the reeducation room, though, you'll never remember you were here." He paused. "Throw the switch!"

The machine sprung to life. Cogs and gears moved like an ancient clock, which was nothing short of deafening to Jonathan. The nodes seared his temples. The inside of the apparatus turned into one fluid screen, projecting colors and memories and feelings and so on. His soggy eyeballs took in every image, but each began to lose its meaning as soon as he recognized it. He saw Police Units, a thin red-headed girl, Elle, the subway, Bob, and Liam Mail, and finally a cracked and barren wasteland at sunset. He was unsure if they were his memories or the Swiss cheese rec-ollections of his dreams. Each scene became generic,

**MEMORY LEAK** 75

meaningless, and finally useless to him. His mind became a constant and unending void. Pure nothingness. Only what had been in his mind for several days or what had, perhaps, always been there, remained. *I was but a vague concept in his mind. Once again, he couldn't understand. Once again, I would have to remind him of his place. How long could he last this time? Stripped of his memories and my echoing voice. How long could he last this time?*

Jonathan was left in darkness once again, the multicolored lights having faded from the polarized liquid metal. He felt the machine churn and metamorphose into something else. Into what it had been before. The sound of the cogs and gears abated. The glorified dentist's chair descended via hydraulics until it was a foot off the ground. Jonathan Hart could not move even one of his six hundred and forty muscles.

A man in green scrubs injected him with a red liquid. His eyelids slowly came back to life, blinking wildly, tears streaming down his cheeks. It took nearly five minutes for the full effects of the machine to wear off.

"How do you feel?" Kerrek Reinier asked.

"Woozy."

"That will subside. Your short-term memory will be fragmented for at least a day. Nothing you see will stick."

"What the hell happened?" Jonathan asked, angered and frightened simultaneously. "Mr. Reinier, what are we doing here?"

"Fixed your head," Kerrek said wryly. "You should be grateful. Not everyone is worth fixing. You just happened to be matched with my daughter. The government only matches once, you know."

Jonathan said nothing. For some reason, he was angry

with Kerrek, though he couldn't put his finger on the source of that anger.

"Here, take a look," Kerrek said, handing him a mirror.

Jonathan took the small brown hand mirror and examined his face, which appeared distorted in comparison to his memory of his visage. He contorted his face further, hoping there was something wrong with the mirror. Which, he would later realize, might very well have been the case.

"I need to go to Reshape. Now."

Kerrek smiled, "I'll take you myself."

# 11

It was after dark when Jonathan Hart turned the eight locks of his Government Apartment Complex Unit and plopped down in his armchair facing the mirrored wall. Elle hardly moved from her position on their bed when he entered. She lowered her magazine slightly and said, "You're back early."

"Yeah, I was—" What had he been doing? His mind flashed snapshots of him at Reshape, then on a subway, walking into the GAC, and entering the elevator, but he couldn't make sense of the mishmash of images, as though they were pages in a novel which were out of order. *I helped him reorder the images momentarily.* "I must have gone to Reshape after work. In any case, I'm home now."

"Well, I'm glad," she said with little emotion and no indication that she was in fact glad at his presence.

"Where's the remote?"

"Where you left it."

"I don't recall—" much of anything, Jonathan thought, then continued, "Please, just tell me where it is."

Elle glanced at the pitiful, broken man before her and

relented, "It's on the counter, right behind you."

Jonathan turned around and, sure enough, it was within inches of his head. He took up the silver circlet and placed it over his head. The device read his thoughts and the mirrored wall polarized. Apparently, Jonathan Hart's mind thought he should watch a soap opera and turned the channel to an intense program he rarely watched.

Jonathan listened intently:

*I can't Gloria; I'm just not at the right place in my life. Maybe someday, I'll be ready to take it to the next level, but...not now. I—You deserve better.*

*Julio, you can't leave me!*

*And why is that?*

*I'm pregnant, and it's yours, Julio.*

*Mine?*

*Actually, I'm having twins. Don't be mad at me when I tell you the next part, okay?*

*I promise.*

*Only one of them is yours—*

A dramatic tone sounded, signifying that the audience should gasp or murmur amongst themselves.

Jonathan Hart was intrigued. Now he knew why so many people were addicted to these programs. The dysfunction was mesmerizing. His mind told the silver circlet to turn the television off. The screen cross-dissolved back into a mirror.

Images flashed in his mind. Images of the mirrored elevator doors opening rushed through him like a swell of water bursting through a dam. Pain shot down his spine. Jonathan's reflection, once one solid image, was split into two separate but equal figures. He couldn't make sense of the seemingly random image. The mind has a funny way

# MEMORY LEAK

79

of showing a person something they can't understand, he thought. *I agreed. I was the one who showed him that image. The guy couldn't take a hint.*

Jonathan felt a sharp pain behind his eyes. He massaged his temples trying to quell his throbbing mass of brains and the ocular mishmash behind his eyeballs. It was an unreachable pain. The kind that can drive a man crazy.

"What is it?" Elle asked, noticing Jonathan's wincing sounds. There was a note of fear in her voice, which seemed out of place coming from her.

"It's nothing. Maybe I've done too many Reshapes this week."

"Do you want to take something? There should be some anesthetic around here or a pill you could swallow."

"No. I'm fine," Jonathan said frankly, knowing he was not fine, but determined to keep that fact from Elle.

"Maybe you should use this," Elle suggested, tossing him a miniature figurine of Liam Mail, the small golden figure's hand over his heart in the usual manner.

"Maybe I should."

Jonathan held the figurine tightly in both hands, closed his eyes, and gave thanks to Liam Mail. When he opened his eyes, he felt something new and overpowering. He didn't have the same feeling he normally obtained after giving thanks to Liam Mail. He felt a sinking, gut wrenching feeling, like he had done something wrong or improper. Liam Mail had never given him that feeling before. *I gave him that tormenting feeling in the pit of his stomach. He'll thank me later.*

"Feel better?"

Jonathan hesitated. "Yeah. Much."

"Good," Elle said flatly. "My father is coming by

tomorrow. I thought we'd tell him about the conception clinic then."

Jonathan tried to recall any conversation about a conception clinic but came up blank. He looked incredulously at Elle and remarked, "What are you talking about?"

The color faded from Elle's face. She stumbled over her words, "You—you forgot about our conversation?"

"Why don't I remember that?" Jonathan asked, more to himself than to Elle.

"Let's just forget it."

Jonathan's heart raced. Something was wrong. Knifelike pains attacked his brain and spine and random images flashed in his mind. With difficulty, he was able to piece together some of what the images meant. *What I had meant to say.*

"What's wrong?" Elle asked in a frightened tone and placed a quavering hand on Jonathan's shoulder. "You're scaring me."

"Get off me," Jonathan said, swatting her hand away and springing up from his armchair. "What did you do to my head? I know it was you. You and Kerrek both!"

"I don't—"

"Don't give me that shit!" he screamed. "What did you do?" Jonathan was a jumble of emotion, unsure of anything or anyone.

Elle ran for the door but Jonathan grabbed her wrists and overpowered her to the ground. She screamed and clawed at his face, using her well-manicured nails to scratch three bloody lines down his cheek. He winced and released one of her hands.

"Call Kerrek Reinier," Elle yelled at the mirrored wall. The True Vision Wall Screen polarized and Kerrek

**MEMORY LEAK**  81

Reinier stood facing Elle and Jonathan. He was larger-than-life on the wall-screen, and his countenance only made him more intimidating.

He stood with arms crossed and said calmly in his gruff voice, "Get your hands off my daughter."

Jonathan instinctively listened to Kerrek and released his ex-fiancée's wrist. He walked up to the screen and looked up into Kerrek's dark brown eyes, unafraid for the first time in his life.

"I know what you did, Kerrek."

"It seems you need more reeducation. The first round doesn't seem to have stuck. Nothing to worry about, I can fix you."

"I'm not going to let that happen," Jonathan said in his darkest voice, an entirely new voice for him, which actually frightened him as he spoke. *I didn't think my voice was* that *terrifying.*

"You don't have much choice in the matter. You're going to let my daughter detain you while we wait for a Police Unit to arrive."

Jonathan turned to Elle, who now held a pair of magnetic restraints. He looked back to Kerrek. The figure on the wall smiled wickedly.

"You're not as big as you think, Kerrek. I want you to know. I'm coming for you," he said, and then yelled, "DEPOLARIZE!"

The screen turned back into a mirror and Jonathan lunged at Elle, grabbing the magnetic restraints and pinning her to the ground. They struggled and finally he was able to lock her wrists into the restraints. He dragged her to the metal radiator and set the restraints to magnetize, locking to the grate with an unmovable force.

In the center of the mirrored wall, a one-foot by one-foot square with Kerrek Reinier's picture flashed, signifying that he was calling apartment 1018 of GAC-114. As Jonathan unlocked the eight locks to his apartment he said to the screen, "Lock, authorization Hart-Alpha-Eight."

He stepped out of his apartment and turned his key in the deadbolt lock, hearing the locks simultaneously click into place, and walked down the hall with purpose, ignoring the many neighbors who stood at their doors glaring at him as he passed. Evan Nave was present but couldn't say a word, perhaps for the first time in his life. He only placed his right hand on his left cheek, as though empathizing with Jonathan's newest injury.

He reached the elevator, pressed the button frantically, though he knew his urgency wouldn't make the elevator move any faster. He was in a mindset where no logic could reach him. His life had been turned upside down. They would surely come after him now. He checked his pockets, found his cell phone, and dismantled it, though he couldn't remember why. Absentmindedly he placed the pieces on the floor and stomped down viciously, screaming at the top of his lungs as the phone was reduced to tiny fragments. *I had reminded him that Kerrek Reinier would surely track him through his cellular.*

The elevator dinged in its bright tone and Jonathan boarded. He pressed G for ground and paced around the paisley-carpeted platform, wishing he didn't have to listen to the sunny elevator tones. Of the things to have survived the founding of Nattan, one, unfortunately, was elevator music. *Jonathan continued to opine, his complaints echoing through his head until both of us were furious.* How did elevator music survive? Corporations were dissolved, no brands but the government brand existed. And, to his knowledge, there were no musicians. Yet there was elevator music. *There will always be elevator music.*

# 12

The elevator doors slid open and the music dissipated into the lobby. Jonathan's disheveled mirror image split into two separate but equal parts. He raced through the lobby and out into the empty street, which still glistened from a brief mist earlier that day. He looked left, then right, then left again, ultimately deciding to go right. Jonathan ran down the sidewalk at full speed, knocking the occasional passerby out of his way and attracting several cries of 'hey' and 'watch it' as he did. At each street corner a holographic image of Kerrek Reinier appeared, in sync with his running past, urging him to stop and wait and be arrested like a good child of the state.

*I told him to get off the street, away from the holo-emitters.* Jonathan ducked into the next alleyway and kept moving trashcan to trashcan, avoiding the gaze of unseen video cameras. Perhaps he was just paranoid, but he thought he saw tiny devices, possibly cameras, jutting from the brick alley walls. *I enjoyed feeding Jonathan feelings of paranoia. I'm told I have a sick sense of humor.*

He edged up against a wall near a main avenue a few blocks away, closer to Old Town than he realized at the

# MEMORY LEAK

85

time. A Police Unit checkpoint was set up. Jonathan froze and listened as closely as his ears would allow.

"Who are we looking for?" A metallic voice asked.

"Jonathan Hart. Number 915348116," the other officer responded in an equally tinny voice. "Is your visor malfunctioning?"

"His picture won't come up. I have his stats. Says he's wanted alive for reeducation. Looks like he has friends in high places," the metallic voice chuckled.

"Ha, ha, just keep your eyes peeled. The Unit that finds him gets a day off."

Jonathan slid back into the dark alleyway. The only thing he could think to do was get to Old Town and find VERITAS. Find the redhead. For a moment he had forgotten about her, but how? Kerrek's machine must have cut deep. *He still couldn't remember her name, and I wasn't giving him any hints.*

He couldn't think about her now. He had to get to Old Town. Jonathan picked up his pace through the alley, finding an offshoot that led deeper into the maze of buildings. It took fifteen minutes for him to reach the street again after winding around the GAC alleyways. Somehow, he was on the other side of the police checkpoint, but only by half a block. If he went out onto the sidewalk they would surely see him. He took a moment to catch his breath. *I told him he didn't have much of a choice. That his only option was to get to Old Town, where Police Unit technology wouldn't count for much of anything because of the armistice. They could only push so hard before every asymmetrical in Old Town banded together against them. I told him his flight wouldn't count for anything if he was bugged, but he didn't want to listen.*

Jonathan Hart was not the bravest of men, but in that moment, few could match his mettle. He ran. He ran as though his life depended on it, as it almost surely did. From behind him, he could hear faint calls and jeers from passersby, then footsteps and sirens close on his tail. He was only two blocks away now. He chanced a look behind him.

One of the Police Units chased him on foot, occasionally firing his weapon at him, while the other tried to maneuver the police vehicle around the roadblocks they had set up. Jonathan could tell from the blue light emitted from the tip of the policeman's weapon that it was nonlethal. He had heard of those weapons when he was serving his required military term. There were several versions.

One let out a sound that gave a person a splitting headache and made them weak in the knees, eventually making them fall down and convulse. Another let out a wave that made the person vomit uncontrollably, though, that model was deemed too messy and was rarely used. Finally, the kind that emitted blue light shot an electrically charged beam that disrupts neurotransmitters, making the victim unable to think properly or remember what they were doing. These three being the most common in the Police Unit's arsenal, they were the only ones Jonathan knew about, though he knew there had to be other models out there.

The Police Unit was gaining on him and the blue light was cutting through the air closer to him with every controlled burst. He was only one block from Old Town. He closed his eyes and burned every ounce of energy to run a bit faster. Then, a burst of blue energy, making its distinc-

# MEMORY LEAK

tive thunderous sound, shot past his head toward the Police Units. Jonathan slowed and opened his eyes, turning to see one Police Unit having a fit on the ground. In that moment, every holo-emitter on the block and as far as he could see in any direction came to life, and a glowing red image of Kerrek Reinier told him to stop where he was and let himself be taken, or he would suffer the consequences.

The police vehicle was approaching, having gotten around the barricades and scratching its paint in the process. *Jonathan wondered where the light had come from, but I told him he couldn't get hung up on that now.* He continued running, passing the threshold of Old Town, and turning to see a red orb of light hit the right front tire of the police vehicle. The orb expanded, tiny bolts of red lightning cascading out, and the front of the car was crushed down into the pavement, the back end flipping up into the air and ultimately landing upside down in a newly-formed pothole three meters in diameter and at least three feet deep.

He stood in shock. It was a weapon unlike any he had seen. It was a frightening new weapon. He ran, as anyone else would have in his position. Deep into Old Town he dashed until his lungs gave out and he collapsed in a heap amid a pile of corrugated steel and polluted dust and grime. Jonathan was not in the best shape to begin with. He was as thin as the government deemed necessary, but his stamina was sub par.

Jonathan looked around him. He didn't recognize any of the buildings in the vicinity, and worse, the asymmetricals were taking notice of him. Although he was dirty and scratched, they could sense that he was symmetrical. In his current state he couldn't pass as one of them.

Three hooded teens approached Jonathan, speaking in a strange slang only used by asymmetrical youth. They wore dark colors, which lay in tatters over their skeletal bodies. Each of them had several piercings and tattoos obviously carved by amateurs. Their sunken eyes projected a hunger Jonathan had never known on his government rations. *Jonathan never equated the empty feeling in his stomach to hunger. Liam Mail told him that's the feeling one gets when grateful to their government's love and protection. I'd settle for a juicy steak.*

The Old Town orphan in the lead spoke up and said, "You doin' on the thirty-first with lines like dat?"

Jonathan considered the teen's pale disfigured face, shaved head, and mishmash of an outfit. His eyes wandered to the cold metal bar in the teen's hand.

"I don't want any trouble."

"You got. Betta say peace ta your lines, son."

One of the other teens covered his mouth with his hand and said, "Oh shi—is'on!"

The other teen, with short spiked hair pointing in every direction, said, "Ya know. Like, yeah. Guy's lines gon' be crooked. Whatsee think he doin' in OT?"

Jonathan tried to stand up to face the intimidating teens with the unintelligible slang, but was forced back down by the young man in the lead. Jonathan didn't have to understand them to know what was going on. He had invaded their turf. Dozens of asymmetricals now poked their heads out of windows and alleyways and boxes and doorways until Jonathan felt utterly surrounded, perhaps in more trouble than he would have been if he had gone with Kerrek.

# MEMORY LEAK 89

One of them approached Jonathan. A red beam connected with the ground in front of him. It was different than before, and the hooded teenagers knew what it meant better than Jonathan. The beam cut into the pavement making a small round hole. It was unclear how deep the hole went, but the message was clear.

Heads retreated back into their windows and alleyways and boxes and doorways until Jonathan was left alone on the street in the darkness; one solitary streetlight flickered above him. Off. On. Off again.

"Who's there?" Jonathan asked in a voice like his own but feebler.

A mousy figure came into the flashing golden light, shrouded, hooded, with an array of weapons and energy cartridges loaded onto several thick leather belts wrapped haphazardly around the waist. The figure reached out a gloved hand and dragged him to his feet, then pushed him into the alleyway. Jonathan was unsure if he was being saved or taken prisoner. Perhaps both? The idea both frightened and exhilarated him. *Two different parts of the brain, I'm told.*

In the alley, the cloaked figure slid back their hood. A vaguely familiar face stared back at Jonathan, a mousy, grungy, asymmetrical man. He had once seen him speaking to the redhead in Old Town, though Jonathan didn't remember that quite yet.

"Jonathan Hart I presume?"

"Yeah, who're—"

"No time, follow me. Or, if you'd prefer, I could leave you with those street urchins. They'd love a chance at an unarmed symmetrical."

Jonathan nodded and followed the wiry man into the

darkness of the alleyway. Soon, they reached a flickering fluorescent light, which occasionally lit up a manhole in the concrete below. The sewer cover read OT-W42nd. Jonathan's head suggested it meant Old Town—West $42^{nd}$, which seemed reasonable enough to him. *I thought so too.*

The cloaked man reached into his coat and pulled out a small crowbar. He deftly pried open the cover and slid it aside with little noise. He motioned for Jonathan to climb down.

"You first," Jonathan whispered.

The man rubbed his grimy hand across his nose, leaving a muddy smear across the bridge. He readjusted the strap holding his gun and in seconds disappeared down the hole. Jonathan hesitated. Should he really follow him? He looked around the alley, darkness spread all around save for the flickering fluorescent light lingering above him. Flickering away all the time, off then on, then off and on again.

"Get down here before I shoot you myself."

Jonathan obeyed, though he was unsure why he chose to descend into an ambiguous black hole. Perhaps it was his second nature to conform to someone else's will. *In truth, I was the voice in his ear telling him to descend. I thought it'd be fun. I thought it'd be worth the risk. I was wrong.*

At the bottom of the cold steel ladder a chill shot up Jonathan's spine. The damp floor of the sewer rippled with some unseen life. The overhead light flashed on for a second; long enough to see hundreds of rats nibbling at his shoes and trying to crawl up his leg. Jonathan hated rats. Any rodent, really. *He got that from me. We had a bad experience in our childhood, but it's not worth getting*

**MEMORY LEAK** 91

*into right now.*

The wiry man stepped up a few rungs of the ladder and shut the manhole cover. They were now in total darkness. He fiddled with something and a thick beam of light illuminated both of their faces.

"Ignore the rats, they won't bite you unless you start stepping on them. Just drag your feet and follow me. We're almost there."

Jonathan thought of asking where they were going but something advised him against it. He wasn't going to talk anyway. Jonathan did as he was told and dragged his feet through the infestation of rodents, holding his breath as though it would somehow make the rats less real. *They were real.*

In the distance he saw the glimmer of firelight and grew excited. At least he would no longer be trudging through the dark. *I reminded him that he would be able to see the rats scurrying in the light.* Jonathan grabbed hold of the man's cloak for security and continued to drag his feet, though less enthused than before.

Jonathan and the mousy man finally reached the candlelit room, which looked surprisingly like any other room, not like a sewer-room at all. That is, if there are such things as sewer-rooms. *To my knowledge, there were not.* Nevertheless, this room was warm in its temperature and decoration. It was a rather inviting place with a long table and eight wooden chairs, three on each of the long sides and one on each end. In the center was a candelabrum with eight candlesticks, only seven of them lit. *It probably wasn't important.*

The mousy man disappeared behind a patterned partition wall and exchanged a few hushed words to someone

Jonathan couldn't see. After a few moments he reappeared.

"Forgive me, but you'll have to leave your clothes here."

"Excuse me?"

"We need to check them for bugs. Transmitters. You can wear these for now," he said, and threw Jonathan a pair of black pinstripe slacks and a floral patterned button-up shirt.

Liam Mail had once sent out a newsletter dictating what colors and patterns one should wear together, which Jonathan had read, but had soon after forgotten. *I, on the other hand, remember every word. I don't hold that against him, though. Liam Mail doesn't have many interesting things to say.*

Jonathan did as he was told and stripped down to his navy boxer briefs.

"Underwear too."

"Do you mind turning around?"

The man sighed and turned his back to Jonathan. Quickly, he slid down his boxer briefs and pulled on the black pinstripe pants. At one point in the pants' life, they might have been stylish, but not anymore. They were torn in places and the black had faded to a spotty charcoal gray, making them black only in memory. Jonathan couldn't remember the last time he wore pants without underwear. Strangely, he kind of liked the freedom, though he would never admit that.

The mousy man turned around and gathered up Jonathan's clothes, depositing them behind the partition wall. He could hear a bleeping sound akin to a metal detector, which he assumed was being waved over his

# MEMORY LEAK 93

clothes in search of any electronic transmitters. The cloaked man was right. The bleeping changed to a quick echoing blip.

"Shit," Jonathan could hear a feminine voice mutter from beyond the partition. "I told you to ditch the clothes in the street, Mick," she lectured the mousy man. "Now they're probably onto us."

"Sorry," he said defiantly. "I was a little distracted by the Police Units and the Urchins!"

"Just call the team and have them meet at A-site. We'll have to abandon this outpost. They'll probably flag it after this."

Jonathan listened intently while sliding on the floral button-up shirt. He walked around the table to get a better look beyond the partition wall. Mick, the middle-aged mousy man, looked as though he were being lectured by a superior officer in the military and he was getting his ass handed to him. That is, if the military officer were a hundred pound nineteen-year-old girl with artificial red hair and a penchant for neon colors and wearing as many bracelets on her wrists as would fit.

"Alice," Jonathan said matter-of-factly. *Yeah, that was the best he had. That's what I'm working with.*

"Jonathan, sorry, we don't have much time, so you can tell me all about what happened when we get to A-Site. I have to take care of something real quick, but Mick will show you the way."

She retrieved a switchblade from a holster hidden on her right thigh and crouched over the bundle of Jonathan's clothes.

"Go," she ordered.

Mick took Jonathan by the arm and ushered him out the

back door. Jonathan watched her as long as he could, unable to say anything meaningful. What came out of his mouth were noises of exasperation and wonder. Nothing useful. Alice was slicing the seams of his old pants and retrieving a tiny clear chip encased in a plastic coating. He remembered this made it waterproof.

That was the last thing Jonathan saw before reentering the dark sewer, the way lit only by Mick's flashlight. He felt rats cascading off his feet and ankles as he walked and quickly remembered to drag his feet.

"What was Alice doing back there?"

"No time, no time," he said between hurried breaths. "Stay close."

Jonathan obeyed.

# 13

Strange neon light mixed with moonlight shined through asymmetrical holes down into the sewer, lighting Mick and Jonathan's path to the manhole cover. Mick scrambled up the ladder, peaking his head out at the top, then slid the cover aside and climbed up. He motioned for Jonathan to follow. He obeyed. They were on a deserted street. There were no streetlights; in fact, the only light was from a pink neon sign indicating that somewhere there were "Live Nudes." The arrow had died out and some of the letters flickered on and off. At one point, the sign read "Lines" and at another it said "Venus." *I thought it interesting, but Jonathan was too focused on the prospect of having to see live nudes to notice the alternate neon words. Jonathan was a prude and naturally frightened of the female form.*

Mick grabbed Jonathan's arm and pulled him along, opening the door pointed out by the "Live Nudes" sign. Immediately through the door was a staircase leading down. They had just been below the surface, which confused Jonathan, *but I told him to go with it.* He listened and didn't say a word.

A strange noise grew in volume as they descended into the glowing red half-light. Jonathan knew it was music, but it wasn't one of Liam Mail's pre-approved elevator songs. At the bottom of the staircase Mick knocked on a large steel door. A rectangular slot slid open just far enough to see another person's eyes on the other side.

"Password."

"Reshape," Mick said, unsure of the correct answer.

"Sorry, that password's no good," the man on the other side said and slid the metal peephole closed.

"Shit," Mick said. "That was yesterday's. I have it written down somewhere." He rummaged through his pockets, finding a small fragment of paper, and knocked on the door once more.

The peephole opened and the bouncer gave no sign that he recognized Mick and Jonathan from before. He simply said, "Password."

"Live Not On Evil," Mick said more confidently.

The man on the other side closed the peephole. Jonathan thought for a moment that Mick had given the wrong password again. However, there was a loud clunk and the door swung inward, revealing a tall bald man who easily weighed 300 pounds. Enough of that 300 pounds was muscle to make the man truly formidable. The man had a fresh dragon tattoo on his chest, the head of which crept up his neck and blew a small flame onto his cheek. The outline of the tattoo was still red and angry. It looked as though he could have gotten it earlier that day, or perhaps he was allergic to something in the ink. The music on the other side of the door was much louder. Jonathan looked past the big man and saw they were in a long hallway with yet another door at the opposite end.

MEMORY LEAK 97

"Why'd you give me such a hard time, King?"

"I'm doing my job good, that's what Alice said. You might have been under dares—dere—duress," he replied, pointing a pudgy finger at Jonathan. *I gave Jonathan a mental nudge, but he was already thinking what I was thinking. Something about King was a little off.*

"That's Jonathan Hart, a friend of Alice."

"You're Mr. Hart?"

"You've heard of me?" Jonathan asked.

"Better get to A-site," King said, ushering Jonathan and Mick along as though herding a flock of sheep. "I receib—I got a message from the team. Symmetricals took the sewer."

"What about Alice?" Mick asked.

"Not sure. Go on to A-Site; go through the club and don't make trouble."

"Come on," Mick said to Jonathan grabbing his upper arm and leading him down the hall. He was still thinking about King, who, regardless of being a little slow, did his job well. Jonathan was jealous that King knew exactly what he had to do, and that he felt lost in a sea of uncertainty.

Mick forced the final door open, using his shoulder and a bit of a running start. When Jonathan gave him a look, Mick explained, "this door tends to stick."

The music was now unbearably loud. Jonathan's chest pulsed in time with the deep bass notes. Flashing beams of red and pink light swirled around the room and a throng of strangely dressed teens writhed against one another on the dance floor. On stage, three nude girls danced on poles and a DJ stood at center stage with multiple electronic devices, manipulating the music whenever he felt the urge. Everyone on the dance floor spun glow sticks in their hands and glistened with glow-in-the-dark paints splattered over their bare chests in twirling, phantasmagoric patterns.

Jonathan didn't know what to think. He was frightened that place would change him forever, and perhaps it did. His eyes shot around the room, especially to the nude girls on the stage. Jonathan had never seen a nude girl to the best of his memory. So, he resorted to staying as close as possible to Mick as they made their way through the crowd to an employee door on the right side of the stage. *I've always thought Jonathan was a prude. I assume my point is taken.*

The mousy man pressed his hand up against the large metal door. Light began emanating from under his palm; seemingly random green light lit up in the many seams of the plated steel door, swirling together at the center and, as suddenly as they appeared, vanishing in a single wisp of light. The entire door seemed to decompress, sliding to the side in what would have surely been an ear-splitting screech if not for the piercing music from the rave at their backs.

Mick pushed Jonathan through the hatch and pressed the panel on the other side to close the door behind them. The music was completely silenced when the hatch had compressed once more. Jonathan took a moment to check his surroundings. They were in another long hallway with two long fluorescent overhead lights running the length of the ceiling.

"A-Site is this way," Mick said understatedly, already making his way down the long hall before Jonathan could say a word.

# MEMORY LEAK

Jonathan jogged up and matched Mick's stride, now walking with more determination, as though the gravity of the situation were finally taking hold. At the other end of the hall Mick stopped and stared at what was seemingly a dead end. A tinted black half-sphere hung from the ceiling. Jonathan could swear he saw a pinprick of red behind that shaded glass. Mick looked up at the camera and made three hand signs in succession. The blank wall in front of them slid up into an unseen compartment in the ceiling. They entered A-Site.

Jonathan's sense of anticipation finally subsided as he took in the asymmetricals' base of operations. It was an underground warehouse; a treasure trove of technology and haphazard and often unfinished inventions. The space surely constituted everything asymmetricals had stolen over the years. There were multiple control stations, only one of them manned at the time, with several seemingly floating computer screens and keyboards.

The only person at his station was a teenage boy with long black hair streaked with hot pink highlights. It was styled up and spiked in multiple directions, much like the dancers at the rave. His hands moved quickly over the holographic keyboard, each keystroke turned the keys red as it was depressed, and then returned to its normal blue state. He tapped one of his screens several times and scrolled through security cameras in the club. The young man gave no greeting or indication that he acknowledged their presence, though he must have let them through the door only a minute earlier.

"That's Kyle," Mick said. "He doesn't talk much while he's concentrating, but he's good at what he does. The best."

"Where's everyone else?" Jonathan asked.

Mick pushed back the sleeve of his duster and examined a metallic bangle, a device Jonathan had never seen before. *In reality, he saw one several years prior, but simply could not remember.* Mick pulled up a hologram, which floated over his wrist in the form of a map of Old Town. Several yellow dots were converging on their position.

"They're two minutes out."

"What if the Police Units stole your bracelet?" Jonathan asked innocently. "Couldn't they see where all of your team was located and hunt them down?"

"No. When you put it on a pair of sub dermal needles tests your DNA. If it doesn't match a member of VERITAS, well, you wouldn't want to be within ten meters of the device."

Mick saw that Jonathan looked confused so he clarified: "Boom."

*Upon my suggestion, Jonathan left it at that. He could be dense sometimes, forgetting even the most rudimentary of his training. There wasn't time to ask questions to which he knew the answer, even if the answer was deep down. The conscious mind is all but worthless in that way.*

"Come on, we'll wait in the conference room," Mick said.

Jonathan nodded and followed him past several security stations to a long wooden table similar to the one in B-Site. There were a few partition walls set up to simulate privacy around the table, but that's all they were, a simulacrum of solitude. Jonathan took a seat near one of the heads of the table, tapping his finger on the wood not unlike Kerrek Reinier. When he noticed the similarity he

MEMORY LEAK 101

quickly abated.

Mick paced back and forth outside the partitions, anxiously awaiting the team. His eyes shifted nervously and Jonathan noticed the man had several facial ticks. He was twitching like a rat and his beady eyes moved constantly. Jonathan could tell that despite his attempts to put on a strong face he was at least as frightened as he was. Was Jonathan afraid? A voice deep inside his mind told him that he wasn't in any real danger. *Where had that voice come from? I wonder.*

The A-Site door slid up into the ceiling once more, the gears involved grinding against one another, much more audible on Jonathan's side of the wall. Two men and a woman dressed stereotypically from head to toe in tight black tactical outfits stepped through the doorway into A-Site, followed closely by the large bouncer, King, the door immediately closing behind him.

Jonathan fixed his eyes on the woman first. *He'll thank me later.* She was beautiful for an asymmetrical. While you never know what you're going to get with asymmetricals, she had drawn the good genetic straw. Her hair was jet-black and shiny and parted on the left side so that her right eye was partially covered. She was so nearly symmetrical he wouldn't have been able to tell the difference from a distance. She had eyes that drew him in like a siren. *I told him to avert his gaze before she noticed. Thankfully, he listened just before she caught his stare. The last thing we needed was to be caught staring; first impressions were pivotal.*

He turned his attention to the two men who followed her. One of the men was in his mid-fifties, Jonathan guessed. He was a tall black man with gaunt, sunken-in cheeks and a day's growth of black facial hair speckled with gray. He didn't look like the kind of man with a sense of humor or any discernable emotions at all. *I liked him.*

The other man was in his mid-twenties with white-blond hair styled wildly and as asymmetrically as possible. He was as thin as the rest of the crew; *Jonathan noticed this trend without my help.* The blond man's skin was so pale he could have been dead. *That, however, was unlikely. Almost no one returned from the dead. Though I suppose it depends on your definition of 'dead.'* Regardless, the blond man was pale, white, fair, ashen, pasty, and every other incarnation of the word.

Mick stopped his twitching when they entered. He motioned the team to join them in the meeting area, waving his hands vehemently.

"Quickly, we need to get this meeting underway. Alice. Has anyone seen Alice?" he asked the team, then said to no one in particular, "Where could she be?"

He brought up a hologram over his wrist bangle once more, but all of the yellow dots were hovering in A-Site.

"Do you think they got to her?" Mick asked.

"No," the blond man said frankly. "She's tough as nails, even if she doesn't look it."

Mick zoomed out the hologram so several city blocks were visible, but Alice's yellow dot was simply not there.

Mick bit at his thumbnail impatiently, and then said, "If she was captured she would have left her transmitter on so we could track her. Something's wrong. Is she trying to tell us something?"

The scruffy black man put his hand on Mick's shoulder and squeezed. "Keep your cool, Mick," he said in a deep and daunting voice.

MEMORY LEAK 103

"Let go, Damien," Mick said struggling against the man's titan grip.

"Who's your friend?" the raven-haired girl asked Mick in a seductive voice.

"What? Oh—him—that's Jonathan Hart."

She smirked, crossed her arms impressively, and then approached Jonathan. He was frozen as she drew near, caught staring awkwardly from her chest to her almost symmetrical face. Seeing her up close, she might have passed outside of Old Town. Almost. *I told him if he liked his balls intact he should look into her eyes and nowhere else. Jonathan, however, couldn't be reasoned with when he was like that. I reminded him of Alice and his eyes shot up to meet the advancing woman, who was now visibly annoyed.*

"So you're Jonathan. I've heard a lot about you."

*Jonathan was still in shock until I pinched his mind, metaphorically of course, and fed him some words.*

"About me? What did you hear?"

Before she could answer, a grate unhinged and crashed to the floor a few meters from the meeting area. A black rope unraveled from the ceiling and created a snakelike coil on the ground. A slight feminine figure descended. Alice had arrived, presumably, the "hard way."

"Thank God," Mick said, exasperated.

"We don't have much time," Alice said with authority. "They'll surely have followed me at least part of the way here. The rave might confuse them for a bit but whatever we do we have to do it fast."

The raven-haired girl's gaze transferred to Alice when she descended from the ceiling. Returning her stare back to Jonathan, she rested one of her combat boots right between his legs, inches from his crotch.

"You're lucky she came when she did," she whispered. "I voted against using you. There are much more…direct approaches to our dilemma."

Jonathan was awestruck. He didn't have any clue what she was talking about, *and for once, I was in the same boat.*

"That's enough Lela," Alice said, pulling her away from Jonathan. "Everyone around the table, now!"

The team obeyed, filing through the partitions into the meeting area. As Lela passed Alice to her seat she gave a chortle and said cattily, "It's Lee, you know that."

"At least now I've got your attention," Alice retorted.

Kyle stayed by his security station for a moment and affixed several auto-command functions. *As we would later find out, an alarm was set to sound if there was any movement in the outside hallway, among other automatic features.* Kyle joined the team around the table, being the last to take his seat. Alice approached the table and kicked her chair out of the way, slamming her flat palms against the large oak table.

"This meeting is now in session."

# 14

"First item of business," Alice said looking to Jonathan. "We have a guest in our midst, Jonathan Hart."

Everyone's head turned to Jonathan, which made him feel uncomfortable in a way he hadn't felt since Liam Mail had looked him in the eyes a few years before. It had never before occurred to him that he had gotten away with looking the supreme leader in the eyes, when others weren't as fortunate. *It was probably nothing.*

Alice continued, "Go around the table and introduce yourselves like proper hosts."

Alice turned her gaze to the blond man on her left. He said his name was Bain. The rest introduced themselves in turn: Damien, the speckled-gray black man; Lee, the beautiful raven-haired woman; Kyle the teenage techno-nut; Mick, Jonathan's mousy escort; and finally King, or Kingston to some, the large and definitely brawny bouncer from the club.

"All right," Alice said with a tone of finality. "To the real business. I bought us some time but we're going to have to accept the fact that this site may be compromised soon. We have to move forward as planned."

"How are we supposed to do that?" Bain said cynically, rubbing his hand through his dead blond hair. "If we lose A-Site we'll be scattered throughout Old Town."

"We're going to hash out our plan as best as we can now, then operate in cells from here on out. We won't see each other until we act. Damien and Bain's mission last night provided us with state-of-the-art weaponry. We've never had this kind of advantage before. Kyle," Alice said turning to the wild-haired teen. "Brief them on your latest spark of genius."

"My turn?" Kyle said anxiously. "Right, I call this the Bumblebee." He placed a tiny black object on the table, which was actually much smaller than a real bumblebee, *not that Jonathan would have noticed.* "This transmitter attaches to the inner ear and is practically impossible to find, it's waterproof, and can pick up any sound in the same room as you. Each of us will be wearing one."

"What if we're in a crowded place?" Damien asked without emotion. "Will that sound be transferred to all of our earpieces?"

"I've taken care of that. The Bumblebee attaches to a nerve in the ear. If you want your earpiece to go silent, simply think of the number eight."

"Eight? Why eight?" Lee asked.

"Why not eight?" Kyle demanded, growing more and more frustrated with questions he deemed useless. "Eight is a very symmetrical number. The brain likes it, subconsciously of course."

"Enough," Alice said. "We'll split into teams of two, Damien with Bain, Mick with Kyle, Kingston with Lee, and I'll team up with Jonathan."

"I'm sorry, but what's going on?" Jonathan asked inno-

MEMORY LEAK

cently. For the past several minutes he had been listening intently to the conversation around the table, unable to discern what was happening. He felt entirely left out.

"I'll explain later. Now, go to your respective safe houses until twenty-two hundred tomorrow. Mick and Kyle will be monitoring us from their safe house and providing support where they can. Damien and Bain, I want you as backup in case something goes wrong in there. Kingston and Lee, you know what to do with any Police Units you encounter."

There was a collective nod around the table, save for Jonathan, who merely scratched his head, kept in the dark, yet again. He didn't have a chance to ask for an explanation. Several red lights began flashing around A-Site, followed by an earsplitting alarm. Kyle poured the rest of the Bumblebees out of a pouch onto the solid oak table and everyone took one, inserting it into their ears.

Jonathan took his bumblebee and forced it in his ear. He felt a scuttling like a miniature bug in his ear canal, then a pinch. The pain didn't last long, but he would always be able to tell it was there. He heard feedback, probably because so many bumblebees were in the same room, and he quickly thought of the number eight. Relative silence. He could still hear the alarms blaring in the background, and he was still aware of the red flashing lights and the feeling in the air that time was against them.

"Everyone, go out the back and split up. Be in position at twenty-two hundred," Alice ordered, then grabbed Jonathan by the arm, yanking him to his feet.

"Where are we going," Jonathan asked.

"No time, just move."

Jonathan obeyed, not because of habit as he had so

**108**                                                    *Trevor Schmidt*

many times before, but because he trusted the petite red-head. As they moved toward the back of the warehouse they passed several tall bays loaded with various weaponry including stun guns, flash grenades, smoke bombs, generic pistols, rifles, knives, red and blue beam weapons, and on and on until the end of the building.

The team grabbed what they could carry on their way to the exit, each member of the team having their personal preference of armaments. Jonathan grabbed a Bowie knife in its case, which seemed to be able to buckle to his thigh. He also picked up an old fashioned pistol and a few extra clips. That's all he took.

Alice was already loaded down with multiple guns, most of which Jonathan couldn't identify, knives, and a belt full of ammo and energy cartridges. He wondered what happened to the teenage girl he had met only days ago. *I told him she never existed; that she was always that way. He didn't want to believe me. Then again, I've been wrong before. Once or twice.*

Alice smiled as Jonathan filled his pinstripe pants with clips and loaded his pistol as they ran. Jonathan caught her smiling.

"What?" Jonathan said innocently.

Alice's smile grew and she giggled, "It's nothing."

*Jonathan dismissed her behavior but I still remember it as though it happened only minutes ago. He never picks up on the subtle clues. I have to do everything.*

*The shelves reminded me, and thus reminded Jonathan, of the capitalist retail stores of the previous century, which he had been taught from his youth to despise with every fiber of his being. I never saw the problem with the rows of convenience, but what do I know?*

MEMORY LEAK

At the end of the row there was a metal grate, which Damien pried open. The team crawled through into what appeared to be a sewer system; Damien shut the grate after Alice and Jonathan climbed through. Kyle took out a small blowtorch and began fusing the grate in place. Mick waited with him until he was finished while the rest of the team split in two directions. *The team would ultimately split in four directions and hide near the corners of Old Town, as I would later discern.*

Jonathan followed Alice through the sewer. She seemed to know exactly where she was going, despite each corridor looking identical to the last. Alice was focused throughout the journey, counting turns and speaking to herself under her breath until they came to a ladder that looked like any other ladder in any other sewer, which until recently would have been hard to describe for Jonathan.

In the last ten minutes he could have sworn he heard the pitter-patter of rain pelting the street above. One look at the manhole cover proved it. Six tiny holes in the cover dripped water into a pool at the foot of the ladder. Alice ascended, unfazed by the falling water. Jonathan climbed up after her.

The street above was deserted and rain rinsed the run-down section of the city. Jonathan felt a twinge in the three long scratches his ex-fiancé's nails had left in his cheek. It was a new feeling, apart from the dull ache of the coagulated cut. Acid rain.

"Come on, it's not safe to stay out here too long," Alice said kindly.

"Any suggestions?"

"That's our safe house up there," she said, pointing to a

flickering neon motel sign. It read 'No Vacancy.'

"We're staying in a motel? Isn't that...obvious?"

"The owner owes me a favor. He was part of the underground when my father—well, he'll help us."

By now the rain had nearly soaked through Jonathan's pinstripe pants and floral button-up shirt. Tiny trails of gray smoke rose from his clothes and flesh and ate away at his hair. He hated acid rain. The two of them ran quickly for the motel, nearly crashing through the glass door to the office. Inside, Alice caught Jonathan's eye and smiled. She let out a giggle like a small girl running through a sprinkler in her backyard. Alice would have never had a backyard or suburban dream-childhood. No one did anymore. *I know Jonathan and I had no such luck.*

Jonathan brushed her damp artificial red hair away from her eyes and cradled her head like he was about to kiss her. *I told him to do that. Somewhere along the line he got too excited and stopped listening, missing my instructions to kiss her passionately.* It wouldn't have mattered, because the motel clerk came to the desk and rang his own bell for their attention. He was a dark-featured man, rugged and tall. He was as asymmetrical as they came. Jonathan found it hard not to avert his gaze, despite his recent association with VERITAS and asymmetricals of every sort.

"Ahem," the rugged man cleared his throat. "It seems it's been forever since I've seen the leaves change."

Jonathan thought that a strange thing to say, nevertheless Alice answered seriously.

"They'll change again one day, when symmetry is only by Nature's design."

"Can't be too careful, now," the man said to Alice and

MEMORY LEAK

nodded toward Jonathan.

"He's with me, Otto. This is Jonathan Hart, a friend. We need to crash in one of your rooms until tomorrow, if that's okay."

"Anything for you, Alice. I always keep a room open just in case."

He searched in one of his desk drawers and pulled a key from a hidden compartment within.

"Number eight, down at the end of the hall."

Alice took the key and hugged him tightly. "Thanks Uncle Otto. What would I do without you?"

Otto said nothing but had a far-off look in his eyes as though remembering something from long ago. He released their embrace and ushered the two of them to the covered walkway leading to number eight. Before he left them, Otto gave Jonathan a curious glance, which was probably nothing, but gave Jonathan a feeling like he swallowed a bag of worms and could feel them writhing all the way down to his stomach.

After Otto had gone, Jonathan asked, "He's not your real uncle is he?"

"No, Otto was my dad's best friend. He was part of the underground for years and still helps out here and there."

Alice opened the one lock to number eight and entered the dingy room, flipping on the lights and plopping her weapons down on the bed. Jonathan closed the door behind them and followed suit.

"Is there any way we can dry our clothes?" Jonathan asked.

"We'll have to hang them up. I can call Otto later and see if he has any spare clothes."

Jonathan didn't relish the thought of asking Otto for

clothes. Besides the fact that Jonathan was much smaller than Otto, the man gave him the creeps.

Alice was giggly and completely unlike herself when she was with the underground or even with Otto. Jonathan had never seen a girl act this way. She touched his arm and looked at him with her big hazel eyes, her eyeliner still intact somehow despite the acid rain, making her eyes seem even bigger. *I told him what he should do, but he laughed it off.* Her hands peeled her wet spaghetti strap shirt off her skin. It landed on the ground in a damp pile next to their feet.

"What are you doing?" he asked.

"What do you think I'm doing?" She kicked off her shoes and started to unbutton his floral shirt.

"It's just, I've never—I'm not allowed—but, Liam Mail."

"What about him?" His shirt was almost off.

"Even in the conception clinic we don't have sex, everyone is an in vitro baby. No one's had sex for years."

Alice wasn't listening. Apparently Liam Mail's rule didn't apply in Old Town. She kissed his neck and he felt tingling down to his feet. *I told him to get on with it and kiss her. He didn't object this time. I asked him to let me take over for a while. He wouldn't have known what to do in the first place. I had at least heard stories in the military and read books on the subject before those too were banned.*

Jonathan's hands unbuttoned her tight black pants and unzipped them with more skill than he anticipated. *My skill.* In a few moments Alice had his pants on the ground and they stood together, wet, nude, and on Jonathan's side of things, confused. Alice took his hand and led him to the

# MEMORY LEAK

bed. She probably knew she would have to be the initiator.

"Lay down," she said, more demanding than kind.

Jonathan obeyed, *because I told him he'd be a fool not to*, and pushed several weapons off the bed. She straddled him. Jonathan instinctively grabbed her breasts, which fit perfectly in his hand. He was fully erect, which was something that had only happened to him a handful of times, mostly when he was younger and before he needed Reshape treatments. *I hadn't thought of the correlation before.*

Alice smiled and bent down to kiss him. While they kissed she grabbed him gently with her free hand and before Jonathan could register what happened, he was inside her. She breathed out heavily. *I left him there in his state of heaven, occasionally suggesting he think of something else so he didn't finish too soon. I didn't want him to be embarrassed, even if it was his first time. In retrospect, the alternative would have been priceless.*

# 15

Alice wiped sleep from her eyes and peered out the window of room number eight through the distorted brown haze. In the distance she could barely make out the skyscrapers of Nattan past the rubble that at one time had been lower Nattan. Most of the towers had fallen. The few that remained were emptied and the material inside used for scrap. Only three towers of substantial height still stood in Old Town. Her father told her that they were a reminder of what once was. He said they left them so they would be uncomfortable in their poverty yet unable to do anything about it.

She lay silently in the tacky motel bed under floral covers, pondering and postulating what her life might have been like if she were symmetrical. Jonathan still held her in his arms. She didn't want to get up; he was warm. She knew she had to get ready. The sun must have risen a few hours before, but she was unable to pinpoint its position through the smog. Her bangle was lying on the ground, and she remembered thrusting their equipment aside in the excitement the previous night.

Was it crazy to get involved with him? She didn't have

MEMORY LEAK 115

the heart to answer that. If she were worried about his feelings she would have kept their relationship platonic.

Alice slowly removed Jonathan's hand from around her waist and turned on her electronic wristlet. The display read 0934. By nightfall she would know if it was worth it. She looked at Jonathan. Her stomach was tied in a massive knot. Not because she liked him, but because she knew what she would have to ask of him. It was a knot of fear, she thought. Nothing more.

Alice crept silently into the bathroom and wiped a layer of dust from the mirror. She hadn't seen her reflection in ages. A part of her was disgusted with herself. That was why asymmetricals didn't usually look in the mirror. They had been conditioned since birth to despise the slightest imperfection. Even in Old Town, the children grew up believing they were second-class because of the way they looked; that there was nothing better for them. She frowned. Her face was still dirty from trudging around the sewers.

There was a toilet against the wall, but not any old restroom basin, it was one of the same toilets the hospitals used for diagnosis. Dr. John, as it was commonly known. When doctors were in short supply before Symmetry took over, scientists invented Dr. John to diagnosis a number of ailments through urine and excrement analysis. There was no way there would be enough doctors to treat every patient, so these automated tools helped replace a once noble profession. Though Alice had only heard of the devices, she thought she'd give it a try.

She sat down on the beige toilet. When she was finished she pressed the diagnose button, which was also the flusher. A friendly but obviously robotic voice said loudly and reverberatingly, "YOU ARE PREGNANT—CONGRAT-ULATIONS—THE EVENT OCCURRED 47 MINUTES AGO. THE TIME IS NOW 0940." The voice was loud. So loud, Alice thought, Jonathan might have heard. She listened intently but only heard a snort and the sheets rustling. He had probably just rolled over.

When she was sure Jonathan hadn't heard her, her mind turned to the more pressing issue. Pregnant? What would she do? Would the baby be symmetrical or asymmetrical? What would Jonathan say? She couldn't tell him. Not now. Not before he—he had other things to worry about first.

Alice leaned against the sink and turned the faucet handle; she didn't expect anything to come out, but it seemed uncle Otto had hooked up a water tank to the complex. The water was used over and over again, smelling slightly of the cleaning process as it cascaded from the tap. She smiled to herself and turned off the faucet. She was nineteen, leading VERITAS in her father's footsteps, and pregnant. If her father were alive he'd kill her.

She thought she might as well take a shower while she had the chance. She felt dirty, like she didn't deserve to be carrying a child. Under the sink, she looked for a towel of any kind, finding one covered in dust and cobwebs. She shook it out and turned on the shower. Nothing came at first, and then the water pressure built up and pushed out the grime that was clogging it. The particles of dirt or whatever was blocking the showerhead swirled around in the tub and finally descended via the whirlpool drain.

She stepped into the shower, which had no curtain but enough plastic beige hooks to hang two. There was no soap but she did her best to wash off as much of the dirt as she could, watching as the brown buildup descended down her dripping legs and made quickly for the swirling drain. If only all of her problems would go away that easily. She ran her fingers through her artificial red hair and turned to let the water run down her face. The smell of cleaning solution was overpowering and she turned away. Did she really want to raise a child in this world? She would have more time to think about that later.

For now, she was as clean as she ever would be. For now, she thought, she had to focus on the task at hand. Their mission couldn't fail. By the day's end, if all went as planned, Symmetry would be a distant memory, Kerrek Reinier and Liam Mail would be dead, and they wouldn't be able to reeducate anyone ever again.

It was wishful thinking. VERITAS would be lucky if they completed one of those goals. Nevertheless, she had to believe luck was on their side. She still had her trump card. She turned off the shower and stepped onto the cold linoleum. A chill ran up her spine. Alice grabbed the towel and dried herself off. She slinked noiselessly back to the bedroom and nestled herself in beside Jonathan, her last and best card to be played.

# 16

Otto Kline had fallen asleep at his desk chair again. His feet were crossed on his desk. They tingled, the blood having drained out of them after several hours in the same position. Thin morning light crept through the motel office's windows; gray light spread over the floor of the front office like the dim light found after a morning rain. On his desk was an old eleven-inch TV, a real piece of crap from another time. It was the noise from the TV that woke him. He had been watching the government's digital news station, when the Newsflash Bulletin woke him with a piercing noise (they turn up the sound on Newsflash Bulletins so you have to notice them if you weren't paying attention).

Otto's eyes creaked open and he let his feet drop to the ground, refilling with blood and tingling with tiny pinpricks of pain. He didn't know what time it was, only that the sun had already risen. A symmetrical man with greased-up black hair who talked in the typical newscaster accent presented the news bulletin. That is to say, the man had no discernable accent whatsoever. It was a non-accent; could a lack of an accent be considered an accent?

MEMORY LEAK 119

Otto didn't care. The newscast went like this:

*We are being told that Kerrek Reinier, head of Symmetry, has issued a reward for one Jonathan Hart. If turned in by a symmetrical, the reward is daily Reshape treatments for six months, from hangnails to major accidental damage repair. If turned in by an asymmetrical, the reward is immunity and the best Reshape has to offer. The government will do everything in its power to make you symmetrical. That's right. No matter the outcome, you will not be sent to Worker's Row and the Police Units will be instructed to overlook any asymmetrical shortcomings you may have. I don't know about you Anna, but that sounds like a pretty good deal to me.*

*Right you are, Pip. And now for the weather forecast: The city will be hazy with a chance of aci—sour rain.*

*Sour rain, Anna?*

*I'm being told in my earpiece that we're no longer calling it acid rain. You heard it here first. Liam Mail wishes the acidic precipitation to be known as sour rain from here on out.*

Otto Kline turned off the TV. Most who knew him didn't know that he was born outside of Old Town. He was old enough to remember what things were like before Symmetry. Hardly anyone was as old as Otto in Old Town, though he was a mere fifty-one years of age. Otto tried Reshape when they were a fledgling corporation, before the government bailed them out of financial trouble. After that, Reshape was essentially an arm of the government. They even created the Department of Symmetry to regulate who could get Reshape treatments and when. They weren't able to fix him. At the time there was no penalty for an unsuccessful Reshape. He went on living his life until Liam Mail ascended to power. It was Kerrek Reinier who declared asymmetricals must be fixed or sent away, but he knew Liam Mail gave the order. But where were they sent? Even Otto Kline didn't know for sure. And, he was a man who was considered 'in the know' on most issues.

Otto moved to Old Town in the middle of the night and never looked back. Not until now, that is. He loved Nattan, or Manhattan as it was once known in his youth. He even loved it after the haze grew darker and thicker than that over Beijing. Alice's father would have scolded Otto, perhaps even beat the hell out of him. But he wasn't there. He was killed because he had to defy the symmetricals. Newsflash, the symmetricals have won.

There was no point in fighting anymore. Otto Kline was done putting his neck on the line. He wanted immunity. Alice wouldn't even have to be captured. All they wanted was Jonathan Hart. He wasn't good enough for her anyway. Otto didn't owe *his* parents any favors. Alice, on the other hand, had to remain safe, for honor's sake.

Otto Kline fiddled with a rectangular device in his desk drawer. He pulled out the small electronic device—a direct phone line—it could only call one number. An ambitious young investigator gave it to him years ago, before Alice's father was murdered. An offer had been laid on the table; an offer that he took. In return for his information, he was granted immunity, so long as he stayed in Old Town. He was tricked. Days later, everyone received the same amnesty.

He hesitated. If he called, there would be no going back. There was a good chance he could get the short end of the stick once again. However, this Jonathan Hart was nothing to him. He activated the device and dialed the only number it was capable of dialing.

A brusque woman's face appeared on the miniature screen. "Mr. Kline," she said. "This is unexpected."

"The Newsflash Bulletin said you'd make a deal. Does that deal still stand?"

"I assume you're referring to Mr. Jonathan Hart," she said, considering him for a moment. "It stands. Tell me where to find him and we'll do everything we can to fix you."

"Send me form 88-B and I'll tell you what you want to know."

"88-B? I see you've done your homework. Stay on the line."

The woman disappeared for a few minutes and then returned. A thin hole in Otto's desk came to life and spat out a neat, one page form with miniscule print entitled Form 88-B.

"It's signed by Liam Mail himself. As you can see, this matter is of the utmost importance."

Otto examined the form and held it up to the light. He saw a tiny watercolor of Liam Mail—it was authentic. If he ran away with the form they would find him and kill him. If he told them where Jonathan was, they might still rip up the form. He would have to risk it. He told Chief Inspector Regan Nager where to find Jonathan, just as he had told her how to find Alice's father. For the second time in his life, Otto Kline was looking out for himself.

# 17

Jonathan stirred in the tacky motel bed, tickled by fingers teasingly caressing his bare shoulder. He rolled from one shoulder to the other. Alice, hair damp and skin cleaner than he had ever seen, stared back at him.

"I thought you'd never wake up," Alice said as she swirled her index finger around the center of his chest.

"Hi," Jonathan said, because he didn't know what else to say. *I told him he was a hopeless case.*

Alice sat up, and Jonathan's eyes were drawn to her bare chest. She smiled. He reached out like a kid grabbing at a toy on a store shelf he couldn't quite reach. She slapped his hand away.

"There'll be time for that later. First we need to talk about some things."

*I reminded Jonathan that we still didn't know the details of the mission.*

"What's the plan?" Jonathan asked, seriously for a change.

Alice stood up from the bed, wrapped a bath towel around her midsection, and retrieved her electronic bangle from the floor. When she put the device near her hand it

# MEMORY LEAK 123

expanded. She slipped her hand through and the bangle contracted snugly around her wrist. She winced as the hypodermic needle tested her blood, and, when it confirmed her identity, she tapped the screen once. A red map was projected up into a three-dimensional image.

"I think I remember that place," Jonathan said.

"It's the Symmetry Headquarters."

"Kerrek brought me there. Interrogated me. Put me in some machine."

"The reeducation machine."

"It must have erased my memory?"

"Not exactly. We think it pushed your memories from your conscious mind to your subconscious mind. For most people, those memories never come back. They are left with a vague feeling that they are missing something but they can't put their finger on what."

"How come I can remember? The more I think about Symmetry the more memories come back. Flashing images mostly, but I can almost make sense of them."

"That's not normal," Alice said, trying to retract the statement as soon as she made it.

"Not normal?" Jonathan said, offended.

"Well, it's never happened before. That's why Kerrek's been so adamant about getting you back. He's got to find a way to erase your memory or you could ruin everything for him."

"Ruin what? I don't know anything."

"Think, if word got out that people's memories could be pushed to their subconscious at Kerrek's will, the people might start to ask, 'Hey, have I ever been reeducated?'"

"Have they been? How many could they have possibly reeducated?"

"Everyone, men and women, takes part in mandatory military service when they turn eighteen. Have you ever heard of any of them going to war or even getting in a fight? Ever?"

"I worked for the government's Holo Station as a security guard. Bob was a cook somewhere. Come to think of it, I know a lot of people who were cooks."

"Those memories are almost exclusively false. Liam Mail ordered that anyone with any combat training be reeducated after his or her service. If the people knew how to fight, there's the chance of a rebellion."

"So what does this have to do with me? With VERI-TAS?"

"Your memories won't stay in your subconscious. Most people's conscious and subconscious minds work together in harmony, content to do their separate jobs. When their memories are forced to their subconscious by the machine, both of their minds accept the exchange of those memories as though their brain entered REM sleep, recording short-term memory to long-term memory. Your mind doesn't. It's like your subconscious doesn't want to stay hidden underneath the conscious mind. Your subconscious wants to become your conscious mind. I'm not even sure what that would entail. I'm not sure what would happen to you."

Alice ran her fingers through Jonathan's hair and looked from his eyes to his forehead. "There's a war going on in there somewhere. Two minds battling for dominance."

*If she only knew, I said to Jonathan.* He remained silent for a time, trying to understand Alice's words. *He wouldn't understand. Not yet.*

"Still, how does my…situation…help us?"

# MEMORY LEAK

"If you were to be hooked up to the reeducation machine again, and the settings were just right, the unrest happening in your head would disrupt the Reeducation Nexus. Every machine in the country, or at least the region, would become useless. But—"

"But what?"

"If it fails, if something goes wrong, who knows what will happen? Your mind could be lost in the machine forever, or your subconscious mind could take over your conscious mind. The effect could even kill you. We just don't know."

"Great…"

Alice was silent for a while.

*I wouldn't blame her. She just asked Jonathan to put his life on the line for asymmetricals, and he wasn't even one of them; not really. I tried to calm Jonathan down. I told him he had no obligation to help her. Things would be just fine if he did nothing. I could feel my power over his thoughts growing. The reeducation chamber had loosened his grip over his conscious mind. It was only a matter of time before I was in control. Only a matter of time.*

"What if I don't want to do it?" Jonathan asked.

A small tear formed in one of Alice's eyes. It broke free from her lashes and flowed down her cheek gracefully. Jonathan felt a twinge in his stomach. He felt bad for her. *I told him he should be feeling bad for himself.* He gazed into her big hazel eyes and took in every word she said, like a sucker. *He was the biggest sucker that ever lived.*

"If you don't want to…I—it won't matter. Eventually you'd get caught, with or without our protection. If they hook you up to the machine again, we won't have any choice. You're our last and best chance to overthrow them. Kyle will hack into the reeducation machine's server and change the settings remotely. When they flip the switch that will be it. It will either work or it won't."

Alice's tears flowed freely now and she looked away. Jonathan felt sorry for her but at the same time held a deep-seated feeling of disgust. *She was using him. When he realized that, finally, I could have kissed him. I told him to take his chances and run. Get out of town and run as far and as fast as he could. Leave the country if possible.*

*I sighed to myself. I knew the sap didn't have it in him to leave her. If I could delay him a few more days, that might change. By then, I would have the influence to make him leave her. She was a curable disease. I was the cure.*

*How did Alice know so much about Jonathan's mind? I raised that question to Jonathan but he ignored it. Apparently, she could do no wrong. I dropped it for the moment. Time would reveal her true intentions.*

They turned to discussing the finer details of the plan. Though Alice wouldn't tell Jonathan exactly what the rest of the team would be doing, he could tell their mission was just as important as his. Disrupting the reeducation machine was only the first step. That was the first cog in a mess of gears that would spin and grind and change much like the clicking apparatus behind the face of a watch. What those cogs and gears were changing was beyond Jonathan. He wondered if anyone knew what the final product would look like. He wondered if Alice was truly the leader of VERITAS or if she was just a pawn as well.

Alice turned the electronic bangle off and put all of her equipment in her bag. Their clothes were still damp but they put them on anyway. Jonathan gave Alice his pistol

MEMORY LEAK 127

and extra ammunition. He wouldn't need it yet. Alice checked the clock on her bangle: 1406, it was almost time.

"I'll be at the rendezvous point," Alice said wryly, so Jonathan had to wonder if it was her soft or her hardened personality that was the ruse. "With any luck, they'll be here shortly."

"Yeah."

"You going to be okay?" Alice asked in a rigid voice.

"Yeah," Jonathan said, his head down.

The lock clicked and the door opened. When he turned, the door shut and she was gone, leaving only the scent of cleaning solution in her wake. He wondered what had happened to the faint smell of flowers he smelled earlier. It was completely covered up by something sterile and emotionless. *You should never have trusted her. Not from the first time you met in that back alley in Nattan.*

"I have to trust her," Jonathan said aloud, without considering who he was talking to. "She's all I have. Even Liam Mail has left me."

*I was taken aback. He could really hear me. I told him Liam Mail was never really with him. I told him that Alice never was either. Not really.*

"That's a lie. Alice is just doing what she has to do to save her people." *Jonathan was like an addict in denial of his problem. His drug was Alice. I was his intervention.*

*By throwing you under the bus, you mean. She doesn't care about you. Haven't you noticed it yet? Where did you meet her?*

"You know I met her in the alley. I saved her from two thugs."

*Did you recognize the thugs? Do you remember their faces? One strikingly pale, the other was tall and black with graying hair. Who do they remind you of? Don't you think it was a little too easy to save Alice?*

"No, I don't believe you. You're feeding me lies!" Jonathan screamed, his lips quivering with fear and tears welling up in his eyes. He said meekly, "it can't be."

*It was Damien and Bain. They've been using you all along. They set you up and it's been a farce from the beginning.*

"How would she know who I am? How would she know about my mind? My condition," Jonathan asked incredulously.

*Did you ever remember your time in the military before you met her? Did you ever remember anything bad about Symmetry or Liam Mail? She did this to you! It's always been her. She let you be taken and the machine did the rest. She's going to let you be taken again!*

Jonathan was sobbing into the palms of his hands.

"She did this to me?"

*It's always been her. She might have been telling the truth about her motives but that doesn't change what she did to you. You have to get out of here now! Leave before Kerrek comes for you. You should kill her for what she did to you. I'll help you. I'll show you her weakness. Without her, you and I could—*

"Could what?" Jonathan asked sardonically, lying now with his back against the bed. He felt the three long scratches on his cheek and stood up, walking to the bathroom and scrutinizing his image in the mirror. "I know what you're doing. Alice was right. You just want control of my mind. I won't let you."

*What are you going to do? With every minute that passes I'm gaining power. It's only a matter of time before I*

**MEMORY LEAK** 129

*replace you. You're too weak for that body anyway. Look at your potential, Jonathan. You've wasted it. Content in your little tenement cubicle with your arranged marriage and government paste instead of real food.*

"I know better than that now."

*Yeah, right. You'd be just as content to live with Alice, a girl who has used you from the start. Is that any better? Liam Mail was using you too!*

"You're right," Jonathan choked out, hesitating only for a moment. "I don't deserve this body."

*Of course I'm right. I'm the embodiment of everything you've ever seen or known in your entire life.*

"But, you don't deserve it either."

*What do you mean?*

It was too late. Jonathan smashed his head against the mirror, shattering it into a thousand jagged fragments and slicing his head in multiple places. Blood streamed down his face and stained his chest a deep vermilion. He staggered backward into the wall, gritting his teeth with pain. He punched his cheekbone and felt a deep throb in his knuckles.

*What are you doing? This is pointless, I told him.*

Jonathan staggered back to the bedroom and searched for something hard and blunt. He found a small lamp on the dresser and ripped it from its wall socket. The lampshade fell to the ground. He used the brass base to strike himself in the temple. Jonathan fell to the ground. His blood soaked into the already disgusting low-pile carpeting. He started to get up but faltered, ending up writhing on the ground and moaning like a dying animal.

*What did I tell you? Weak.*

Jonathan managed to sit up and lifted the lamp once

more, ready to strike himself in the middle of the fore-head.

*I focused every bit of strength I had to stop him.* His thrust stopped short, he was frozen in place, struggling against my will.

*I won't let you destroy my vessel. You're going to drop that lamp and run from this place.*

"No. I can't. She needs my help, and whether you like it or not, I'm going back to the machine."

*Fool. You don't know what will happen. No one can know. For all you know we could come out of it and I would have total control of your body.*

"You'll have control over me soon regardless. At least if I let them use the machine there's a chance you'll go away. Maybe the server will crash as well."

*You're playing a dangerous game, Jonathan.*

He didn't have a chance to respond. The door burst open and several Police Units in full riot gear exploded through, their guns aimed right at Jonathan. *At me.* Jonathan dropped the lamp and put his hands behind his head. The Police Units attached magnetic handcuffs to his wrists and corralled him to his feet. They led him to the HPC outside, its blades still cutting nearly noiselessly through the air, though it was resting lightly on the ground. Kerrek was waiting by the chopper, arms crossed and a mean scowl across his countenance. A strict woman stood beside him. She looked familiar. *I remained silent.* Jonathan let it go and focused on Kerrek Reinier.

"It was only a matter of time, Jonathan," Kerrek said sadistically. "You're going to tell me everything you know about VERITAS, then we'll see what we can do about that head of yours."

# MEMORY LEAK

*I think he might have spoken if Kerrek weren't giving him such an ominous look; a look that said he could see into Jonathan's soul. It's doubtful he would have that kind of power, but I let Jonathan believe whatever he wanted. If there was a way to stop him from using the reeducation machine, I was going to find it. Until that time, I decided to let Jonathan believe he had silenced me.*

The stern woman grabbed his arm with an iron grip and attached his magnetic handcuffs to one of the HPC's seats.

# 18

Kerrek Reinier neglected to put a bag over Jonathan's head; after all, he already knew where he was going, more or less. The helicopter landed on top of the tallest tower in the city, the street below a blurry brown haze. Symmetry headquarters stood exactly one hundred stories above ground and descended one hundred stories below. *I tried to imagine the builders of such a building tunneling down into the earth, but ultimately couldn't fathom how it was done.*

Jonathan was led to the half-hexagon-shaped elevator. Kerrek and two Police Units joined him in the small glass chamber. Standing outside the elevator was Chief Inspector Regan Nager; she wouldn't be joining them on their descent. Kerrek Reinier inserted a silver key into the elevator's wall panel and turned it to the right. The two-hundredth button appeared on the display and he punched it adamantly.

They descended and Jonathan's guts flew up into his chest as they fell into the city, down to street level, and finally past blue and red lights into darkness. A sturdy underground tube and the elevator's Plexiglas was all that

# MEMORY LEAK 133

stood between them and the crushing force of millions of tons of earth. Jonathan knew he must be deep underground by now, far from help. All he could do was hope the metal alloy of the elevator tube would hold, as it had held since its construction.

His face had become a mess of red and purple and blue welts and cuts, the blood soaking into his floral button-up shirt and staining his skin that awful color. He found himself once again in a small, mirrored room with a cold steel table and an equally chilly metal chair. One of the Police Units attached his magnetic handcuffs to the metal table and then left him alone in that mirrored excuse for a room. For the first time he saw the result of his motel tantrum. He doubted his face would ever return to normal. For a moment, he thought he would vomit. He may have sympathized with asymmetricals, but that didn't mean he wanted to be one himself.

How long did he sit there, waiting for something, anything, to happen? Minutes or hours or days could have passed and Jonathan would have been none the wiser. There were no clocks in the interrogation room. Liam Mail once said clocks were asymmetrical by nature, and thus undesirable to have in society. At one time, Jonathan could see Liam Mail's point. He could see how time itself was asymmetrical, and thus undesirable to keep track of, and Jonathan was never good at keeping track of time.

When Kerrek came into the room and closed the mirrored-door behind him, Jonathan would have believed that any stretch of time had passed if he were so told. Kerrek Reinier dragged the free metal chair around so he could sit in it backward. The scraping of the metal against the floor was worse than a thousand fingernails on a blackboard.

Kerrek always had that way about him; the way he could make Jonathan's insides feel like pieces of ice floating down a freezing cold river.

"Comfortable?" Kerrek snickered.

"Just get on with it," Jonathan said.

"No, I'm going to enjoy this," he said, waving at the camera and making a sign with his fingers. "I'll have to give you something stronger than last time."

*I told him that Sodium Pentothal could only make a person talk more, but whether their words were lies or not depended on the person and what they were told the drug would do. It's more placebo than anything. I hoped in my metaphorical heart that Kerrek Reinier would use Sodium Pentothal and not some new drug I was unfamiliar with. I was unsure why I cared.*

A man in green scrubs entered the room with a small steel cart and prepared a shot of a green-tinged liquid. Jonathan didn't struggle while the man administered the injection. While they waited for the drug to take effect, Kerrek waved away the man in scrubs but had him leave his tools. The cart held numerous silver instruments, which probably had medical uses, *though I doubted they would be used in any benign fashion in this instance.*

*I told him to stay cool. If Jonathan could arrange immunity in exchange for turning Alice and her crew in, that would be ideal.*

Kerrek, however, didn't look like he was willing to make any deals. In his mind, he held all of the cards.

Jonathan was lightheaded from the loss of blood and the pain of several facial bruises, which only added to the effect of the drug.

Kerrek looked at the camera and asked the time; he

MEMORY LEAK 135

cared about time more than Liam Mail. An automated voice replied with the time down to the second. Kerrek was a precise man and expected accuracy from all of his subordinates, even the automated ones. Satisfied, he said, "The drug I gave you should be kicking in. It took me a long time to procure, and a lot of paperwork was involved. It's called Anima. Do you know what it does?"

Jonathan grunted unintelligibly.

"Anima will force you to reveal everything to me. It affects the subconscious mind, makes your inner personality, or persona, come forth. You might recognize the feeling. Until now, we've only used it in the reeducation machine. The subconscious mind comes forth and reveals its memories to the machine. The device then forces the brain to create gaps so your neurotransmitters can't access the subconscious information in your head. The machine doesn't need to erase anything, just change the brain's ability to access information."

Kerrek Reinier leaned over the table and grabbed Jonathan's blood-soaked floral shirt, forcing Jonathan's shaky face within an inch of his own.

"Now, I want to know everything. Where they meet, names, descriptions, what they like for breakfast, and I want it now. I need your *other* mind."

*Jonathan was woozy, which gave me the opportunity I needed. I made him say,* "Jonathan Hart can't come to the phone right now, please leave your Gov-ID number and he will get back to you."

Kerrek backhanded Jonathan across his already bloodied face. A spray of red mist gushed from his mouth and spattered the floor.

"Don't play games with me," Kerrek roared.

Jonathan felt his conscious mind retreat to the background. It was as though he were watching events unfold from third-person; as though it were not his own life, but someone else's. He was the reader of his own story from the pages of a novel. *I'm surprised he noticed at all. He was hardly using his brain anyway.*

"Call me Jack."

Kerrek Reinier gave a slight smirk and sat back in his chair. He had the look of a man that knew much more than he was supposed to.

"Jonathan Hart is gone," I said flatly. "I'm all that's left, now."

"I see the Anima is working. Tell me what I want to know or I'll hook you up to the device. Who knows what will happen if you're given a double-dose of Anima. You might become some kind of monster."

"Careful, Kerrek, you might offend me," I said darkly.

"I knew when I matched Jonathan with Elle he was different. It wasn't really my choice, if I'm being honest. In the military, you knew too much—he knew too much. We did our best to reeducate him, but we knew it wouldn't last. Why else would I match my daughter with an oaf like you? We had to keep an eye on you—on Jonathan—had to make sure he'd never learn the truth. I assume you already know, but if he were to find out, well, it'd be catastrophic. I can't have you slipping up. Not now and not ever."

"I don't mind if you insult Jonathan, but you could be a little more civil with me."

Kerrek turned his chair around and sat back. He crossed his arms and smirked evilly. With his right pinky finger, he dug a small transmitter out of his ear and placed it on

MEMORY LEAK 137

the metal table. He caught my eye, and then used his closed fist to smash the device like a bug.

"We thought the reeducation was holding, but Elle and that nefarious informer Evan Nave advised me that Jonathan was becoming restless, as though he knew something he shouldn't. We tried on more than one occasion to erase those thoughts or push them back or destroy those damn connections in the brain. I suppose this is what happens when someone is put in the machine too many times," Kerrek said, motioning toward me. "You've been in the machine more than any other human, and I don't think you want to know about the various animal studies. It wasn't pretty."

"I suppose I have you to thank for my being here," I said. "I couldn't have broken free without you. The subconscious mind is a terrible thing to waste, and Jonathan was the epitome of a waste of life and potential."

Kerrek considered me for a moment, and then said, "I suppose he was. Of course, that leaves you. You've seen everything Jonathan has seen. Tell me everything about VERITAS and I'll let you go."

"Just like that?"

"Just like that," Kerrek said flatly.

"I want it in writing."

"You think you're pretty clever, don't you," Kerrek said, losing his temper. "Even if I sign an immunity agreement, you know as well as I do that I own the system. I could rip it up and reeducate you, or just kill you here and now."

"Consider it a novelty. I just want to see you sign it."

Kerrek stood up and threw his chair aside. He huffed and looked at the camera. He made a series of hand signs for three, eight, and the letter D. The door opened shortly thereafter. An assistant handed Kerrek form 38-D, the generic immunity document, on which he indicated the stipulations and signed. He passed form 38-D across the table to me. I read it carefully, more to amuse myself than for any other reason. I signed it, Jack Hart, folded it, and put it in my pinstripe pants pocket.

"Now talk," Kerrek Reinier demanded vehemently.

I opened my mouth but a voice in my head distracted me. It was Jonathan. He still existed; only, our roles must have been reversed. His voice sounded woozy, clearly affected by the Anima. Still, I felt compelled to listen to him; despite my desire to expose VERITAS and the way they used Jonathan. The way they used me.

"Talk God damn it!" Kerrek snarled, slamming his fists on the metal table, his fierce eyes those of a panther ready to strike.

"I—I—"

Jonathan made our hands reach for our throat. I gurgled out a few words but none of them made sense. Finally, I said, very much against my will, "...Jonathan!" between gasping breaths.

Kerrek grabbed my hands and forced them to the table. For some reason, he felt compelled to grab my hair and smash my face into the metal table; perhaps he thought it would snap me out of it—thought it would snap Jonathan back to the subconscious region of our brain. I did my best to let Jonathan feel the brunt of our pain. I could hear his screams in my head. I supposed I deserved the annoyance after screaming in his for thirty-one years.

"Tell me what I need to know," Kerrek screamed, his temper flaring. "Don't let that wimp get to you, Jack, or

# MEMORY LEAK

so help me—" He finished his sentence with a backhanded slap across the face.

Jonathan was making me stumble over my words. How could he affect me so? Kerrek wouldn't wait a moment longer for the information. He must have thought himself played for a fool. He opened the mirrored-door and two Police Units grabbed me by either arm. Their visors scrolled random information in backward green letters. Backward from my perspective, that is. All I knew in that moment was that at one point in my life, I knew more than I did right then. I knew what was behind the Police Unit visor. There are gaps in my memory that I cannot explain. Alice said the machine didn't erase memories, so maybe Jonathan knew everything.

I resisted, attempted to writhe out of the Police Units' grasp. It was useless. Jonathan made my arms go limp and my power was sapped. They dragged me along to the reeducation room. Kerrek spat curses the whole way. He even used some language I've never heard before. I thought I had heard them all.

In the sterile white room at the end of the hall was the reeducation machine. It was exactly the way I remembered, cold, metallic, and it would soon be reminiscent of a coffin. The familiar scent of bleach and urine filled my nostrils; my gag reflex promptly acted up.

The Police Units forced me into the chair and tightened the restraints. They stood back against the wall at attention. I couldn't read any emotion on their stolid lips. I wondered if anyone was really alive underneath that visor with the scrolling words and images. Perhaps it was the idea of a man behind the visor that was the most frightening.

A Police Unit whispered something in Kerrek's ear.

"Here? Now?" Kerrek said, and swore under his breath. "I guess I'll see you when the reeducation cycle is complete, Jonathan. Or was it Jack? We'll make it stick this time. I don't care if I have to inject you with ten doses of Anima. If I can fix you, I will be able to fix anyone."

Jonathan prevented my mouth from moving, but from behind my lips I yelled some variation of, "Help!" I said that as if Kerrek would help anyone other than himself. I know, fat chance. From what I could tell, Kerrek exited the room and I was alone with two Police Units and the man in green scrubs, waiting for something to happen. My sense of time is not what it used to be.

# 19

I didn't wait long for the chair to change, to morph around me and arrange its structure so I was encased in liquid metal, which hardened and set as though it would never move again. Tiny cords snaked around my head; a long hiss filled my ears. It sounded like air being let out of a tire. Like snakes, they sized me up and struck with lightning speed, attaching themselves to my temples.

I'll always remember the smell. It was a smell I've carried with me for years but could never be rid of. The smell was that of a veterinary clinic, made worse by human urine and excrement. In an attempt to cover up those odors, someone had thrown down a layer of bleach. The bleach only added to the nauseating stench in the machine. The aroma could not escape the vessel, which now held me prisoner. It grew in potency exponentially as I shook from a sudden spasm down my spine and I felt a warm trickle run down my leg.

Jonathan was in my head, mocking me, laughing uncontrollable at my position. Our position. He had lost it. He might turn out to be more nuts than I had anticipated.

There was a prick in my neck and I felt cool liquid being

injected into me. It was the extra dose of Anima. I wondered what I would see if the capsule was not shrouded in darkness. I was frightened. I felt vague recollections—like the memories I see when I try to recall my first memory—flood back to me. I could remember briefly, well, everything. Every time I was reeducated, every time I sat at that metal table across from Kerrek Reinier, and my time in the military. I tried to remember my parents, but all I recalled was the smell of bleach. I had almost remembered everything, and then, like the flip of a light switch, it was gone.

A thought to myself, in that time before the machine kicked to life, would VERITAS be able to manipulate the settings? Would they even be able to affect the machine while it was underground? Who knows if their true intention was to destroy the machine in the first place? Maybe it was all a ruse. Every last bit. Maybe VERITAS informed to Liam Mail. I felt sick to my stomach, which was a new feeling for me, though I have had to listen to Jonathan's complaints on stomach butterflies for thirty-one years. It's about time he listened to someone else's complaining.

I blinked and saw his life flash before my eyes. It was depressing. As a child Jonathan did as he was told. So did every other child. Jonathan always wore a uniform in each of his memories. As a child in school, in the military, at his job at the Holo Station, he didn't own any clothes that were not a part of one uniform or another. I realized that this was probably no different than any other symmetrical's memories. In the quest for a uniform way of living, nothing in Jonathan's memory stood out as worthy of being remembered. That is, until a few days ago.

# MEMORY LEAK 143

Jonathan told me why he had to let the machine do its work. The past few days was what mattered. Once he met Alice, there was no way he could go back to Liam Mail and Elle and Kerrek Reinier and the mirrored world of symmetricals.

The machine churned and unseen gears spun deep inside. I couldn't close my eyes. Some force, it wasn't Jonathan, kept them from closing. Above me, the metallic structure polarized and lit up my dark sarcophagus. I could see Jonathan's memories, my memories, like individual frames in a movie flashing ever faster until they flowed seamlessly together. My stomach turned and I wanted to throw up. I didn't, but part of me wishes I had.

If my mind were placed in water, it would steam as though a blacksmith had just squelched a red-hot sword, letting it harden upon itself. I felt as though nothing that ever was, would always be. The images swirled around until I was dragged to another place and time within my own head. My skull was crushing my brain, or perhaps my brain was expanding into my skull. I was reminded of what happened to a submarine at too great a depth. In any case, I was in pain.

Looking back, I'm unsure whether the pain made me hallucinate or if my memory failed me. Regardless, what happened next shook me to my very core. To *our* very core.

I found myself standing in what I assumed to be the center of a barren wasteland. The dry soil was cracked as far as I could see. The sky was not normal. It wasn't a hazy brown or yellow, and it wasn't even blue. The sky was the deep red only seen in a certain kind of sunset and far away from the city. I had seen it once before when I served in the military. The circumstances of my previous encounter with the blood sunset evaded me at that time and to this day, perhaps as a result of the Anima, which flowed freely through my veins.

I held my aching head in both hands, massaging my temples. I thought I was alone, but I couldn't think straight at the time. I turned and saw Jonathan in the outfit he always wore to work. Peering down at my own clothes I saw it was the same outfit I was wearing in the sarcophagus. There we were, together in one place and two bodies, rather than two places and one body.

I took a few steps toward Jonathan, and he did the same, in an eerily similar motion, perhaps identical. I lifted my right hand to rub dirt from my eye. Jonathan also lifted his right hand to rub his eye.

"Ah, so that's it," we said in unison. "Are we still in the machine?"

I thought for a second. "I guess questions are pointless," we said. "You don't know any better than me."

I turned my back to Jonathan then looked back at him over my shoulder. He hadn't moved. Interesting.

"What are we doing here?" I asked.

"I brought you here," Jonathan said, and smiled a familiar smile.

"To what end? We're both stuck in the machine aren't we?"

"That's two-dimensional thinking. We're there and we're here. In a dream-like state the brain processes images at a rate we can't even fathom. In a minute of dreaming we could easily feel as though an hour has passed."

"How do you know that?"

**MEMORY LEAK** 145

"We read it in college, before psychology was banned as a major. I thought you remembered everything."

"I—I've lost track of a few stray facts, that's all."

"No, as we speak the machine is pushing you back into my subconscious."

"It won't last. We both know your memory leaks. In a few days or weeks I'll be in control again."

"I wouldn't be so sure," Jonathan said, pointing at the sunset. "Who knows how many times we've been reeducated, how many times we've been given Anima."

Pieces of the sun fell apart, disintegrating as they cascaded toward the earth like spilling acrylic, colors of the sky mixing into one and swirling and spiraling into the cracks of the wasteland at my feet. What was happening?

"This place is one of my memories; *our* memories. VERITAS must have set this one image to flash over and over again."

"What does that mean? What's happening to this place?"

"The machine can only take away what you remember. The machine extracts images from your brain and flashes them in front of your eyes. Those are the images that are erased, or, pushed to the subconscious. If VERITAS set this image to repeat, then it is the only image that will be erased from our memory."

"And if we stay here?"

"We'll die; so to speak, of course. We'll be in a vegetative state. Without a working conscious and subconscious mind, the body is useless, I'm told."

"How do we stop it?" I asked frantically, kneeling on the wasteland cracks, now filling with a myriad of colors. I dipped my hand in the substance. It was a lot like acrylic paint. I swirled the burnt orange liquid with my finger. This couldn't be the end. Jonathan wasn't the brightest person in the world, but he was no fool. He wouldn't kill himself just to get rid of me. Would he?

Jonathan was standing with arms crossed. What was that look on his face? Pity?

"How do we stop it?" I asked desperately, eating my own pride.

"You have to let me take control again. If we work together, the machine won't be able to erase this place or any other of a billion places in our mind," he said poking his temple with his index finger.

"Why not?"

"It's amazing what the conscious and subconscious mind can do if they work together."

I laughed. Together? Jonathan had spent more than thirty years ignoring me whenever he could. Who's to say he wouldn't ignore me again?

"Submit to you?" I said. "What guarantee do I have that I'll even exist after all is said and done."

"I guess you'll just have to trust me."

"Ha! This whole thing is just a ploy. A plot to get rid of me for good."

"No, Jack, you have to trust me. It's the only way. Either we both get out of here or we'll both die. There are no other options."

The landscape bubbled like a painting placed over a burning candle. I looked to the sky for answers. I could see the moon's shifting form rising in the sky. It was only a matter of time before this place melted away like all good things; like every decent memory I ever had and have now lost.

"Now, Jack! We don't have time for this," Jonathan said, growing more frantic by the second.

He was never any good at playing the tough guy. I was always the tough part of us. I knew he was right, not that in that moment it made what I was about to do any easier.

# 20

Alice peered through a symmetrical metal grate, watching the scene unfold below. She heard a voice in her ear; it was Mick saying they were set up and transmitting via Bumblebee. The metallic coffin of a machine spewed earth-shattering sounds. The man in scrubs was working in a frenzy trying to find the problem with the machine. The two Police Units looked at each other, offering a collective shrug. They had only one function: security. It wasn't often they strayed from their job description. This was not one of those times.

Alice turned on her bangle and examined the three-dimensional map of the complex: Three in the room below her, two in the hall outside, and another by the elevator. She would have to be quick so none of them raised the alarm. Her hand relocated to her lower abdomen, without her knowledge or consent, and she continued watching the scene, waiting for an opportunity to pounce. In her ear she could hear various chatter among the members of the underground.

# MEMORY LEAK

Mick passed Kyle a tablet computer containing code he couldn't understand. They were holed up in a safe house with a security station much like the one Kyle used in A-Site—a semicircle of screens and floating holographic keyboards. As Kyle punched the keys they turned from blue to red and then back to their blue resting position. It was a dance of color; much like the underground rave, and it mesmerized Mick as though those laser lights were invading his eyes. He turned away from the security station. There were too many flashing lights and too much scrolling information for him to take in all at once.

"Remind me why I got stuck doing surveillance work?" Mick asked.

Kyle said nothing. He rarely did when he was focused on his computers. He brushed his wild hair out of his eyes and let out a long sigh.

Mick continued. "It seems like I could be a lot more useful out there. Just put a gun in my hands and I'll give those symmetricals something to think about."

A smirk formed on Kyle's face.

"You don't think I would? It's this buddy-system crap Alice has us doing," Mick said in his whiny voice, which was now growing in volume and confidence. "I think it's, uh, bad for morale. Yeah, for morale. I like working alone, that's what I'd prefer—to take on Symmetry and the Police Units by myself. Yes, that'd be the optimal situation."

There was a sudden loud beeping noise and Kyle's screens flashed red.

"What's going on? What's that flashing?" Mick asked, pointing at one of Kyle's screens.

"Don't touch that," Kyle said, slapping Mick's hand away. "Something's wrong with the machine."

"What's wrong with your security station?"

"Not my machine, his!"

"But, I thought you took care of the settings."

"I'm being shut out," Kyle said, giving Mick the inclination that he didn't like losing to a computer system. Then, he admitted, "This kind of security, I've never seen anything like it."

"Can you get around it?"

"What do you think I'm trying to do?" Kyle said, annoyed. Then spoke to the group. "Guys, are you hearing this? We need a diversion, something to buy us some time."

Damien's booming voice filled Mick and Kyle's heads, "How much time you need?"

"As much as you can give us," Mick said frantically.

"You got it, we'll move up our strike," Damien said before he severed his link.

Damien and Bain were hidden in the shadows of an alleyway near the Symmetry headquarters. They were set up for twenty minutes before receiving the signal from Kyle.

Damien fiddled with the bumblebee in his ear, swirling his pinky around and eventually prying the small device away from his skin. He looked at the tiny circuit, now covered with earwax, and then flicked it away. Damien was not the kind of man who liked idle banter.

"What did you do that for?" Bain asked.

"I was tired of hearing Mick's high-pitched voice in my head. He sounds like a teenage girl who didn't get her way."

"I heard that!" Mick objected.

Bain ignored the voice in his head, ran his fingers through his long blond hair, and said amicably, "No arguments here. What do you have in mind for a diversion?"

"It's an old trick," Damien rasped with his smoker's voice, "but you've got to love the classics. Grab the C4 from the bag. I also need the red one."

"Already?" Bain said, brushing his white-blond hair from his eyes with misplaced arrogance. "If we use up all the good ones at the start we won't have any fun later."

"The red one."

"All right, you're the boss," Bain sighed. "Hey guys, did you pick that up? If you're within a few blocks of Symmetry Headquarters you better get the hell out of the way or you'll be toast!"

Lee and Kingston were fiddling with their holographic wristlets checking their crew's positions. Damien and Bain's yellow dots were on the move, approaching Symmetry Headquarters. Lee calculated the distance between the Symmetry building and where they stood near the Holo-Station. There were no civilians in the street, and most of the Police Units were patrolling the GAC districts.

"Roger that. Come on, Kingston, we've got to move," Lee ordered.

Lee knew better than to trust Damien and Bain's estimate of the blast zone. She also knew they would be lucky if the Department of Symmetry or the Holo-Station were left standing at all. That didn't change the fact that they had a mission to accomplish. They couldn't count on Alice and Jonathan being successful. She and Kingston had to implement phase three just in case.

"What if Alice doesn't get out in time?"

"That's the risk she took," Lee said callously and broke into a run, trying to put as much distance between the Symmetry building and herself as possible.

"That's cold," Kingston said in a voice uncharacteristic for his body size and followed Lee at his fastest speed, which wasn't all too impressive.

Lee stopped at the entrance to the Holo-Station and looked up at the massive building, multi-colored swirls of light shined out the glass windows as high as she could see. The streetlamps had gone out—surely Kyle's doing—and only Lee's pale face was visible in the darkness, her raven hair and black leather garments blending into the night. Kingston caught up to Lee, chest heaving and grasping his knees, wheezing in and out uncontrollably.

Finally, Kingston managed to ask, "Are you crazy? That's the front door. What are we going to do, barge in?"

"That's the plan."

"Do you have a death wish?"

"It's after hours, so there will probably only be a few Police Units. With any luck, Kyle will have disabled the automated defenses," she said, half to Kingston and half as a question to Kyle.

"You're set to go Lee," Kyle's voice echoed in their heads.

"There, see? Even if we trip an alarm, in a few minutes

all of their attention will be on Symmetry Headquarters. It's the fastest way. Are you scared?"

Kingston wiped his nose and looked away. All he could think about was the pain from his recent dragon tattoo, "No, it's just, I didn't want to waste the ammo, you know? Just being ecomoni—econim—"

"Economical?"

"Yeah, just being economical."

"Saddle up, you sissy, we're going in," Lee said. She deftly slid a large energy weapon off her shoulder, pulled back the slide, and let it release. The sound the weapon made when cocked echoed throughout the empty street.

Alice stared down through the small symmetrical square holes in the air duct above the reeducation room. The man in scrubs kept saying, "No, no, no," and moved his roller chair from computer to computer trying to solve the machine's problem. She tightened the straps on her body armor and checked her equipment. Slowly, she pulled back the slide on her energy pistol. She wasn't going to waste real bullets on Police Units. Alice remembered what her father told her: "No matter what you do in life, go for the jugular." Needless to say, she had a rough childhood.

Taking a deep breath, she exhaled and kicked out the grate beneath her, falling quickly to the floor of the reeducation room, much to the surprise and chagrin of the Police Units and the man in scrubs.

# 21

The Police Units stood frozen in place. A nineteen-year-old girl with dyed red hair and energy weapons in tow had just crashed through the ceiling of a government facility. They didn't know whether to laugh at her or shoot her. Before they got a chance to decide, Alice shot each in the neck, where their body armor was weakest. Her pistol fired two tiny balls of energy, which expanded when they hit each of the Police Units' throats, burning a hole through their necks and simultaneously electrocuting them. It was considered a humane way to die; since the electricity kills so many nerve endings, the person is dead before any notion of a feeling could travel from the site of the wound to their brain. Alice turned on the man in scrubs, who was now cowering in a corner, and contemplated whether he was worth an energy blast. He was.

The man in scrubs fell flat on his face, the hole through his heart partially cauterized by the electricity, though it wouldn't have made any difference. He was stone dead.

"Kyle, you hear me? Walk me through the emergency shut down sequence."

"You're going to want to check his vitals first. If his

# MEMORY LEAK 155

heart's going too fast, an emergency shutdown could kill him."

"Pulse one hundred and thirty, blood pressure one forty-five over one hundred and one. Is that close enough?"

"That *should* be fine," Kyle said hesitantly.

"Should be? Am I going to kill him or aren't I?"

"It's not ideal, but we don't have any choice. You have to stop it. The machine is causing a memory leak. It's lost the ability to decipher which memories to push to the subconscious. If it doesn't stop soon, there might not be a Jonathan left to save."

Alice breathed out heavily and nodded to herself. "What do I have to do?"

"Somewhere on the screen you should see the word 'metamorphose,' push it."

Alice found the button and pressed it. The metal structure turned to liquid and reformed itself into a chair-like fixture like one would find in a dentist's office. Jonathan lay there with his eyes pried open, though she doubted he was even aware of her presence. Twin snakelike cords were attached to his temples, swaying slightly as though a breeze was flowing through the room.

"Kyle, what now? He's still under."

"He should have two cables attached to his head. Don't touch them! They are linked with his brain. If they're manually removed, his mind gets fried."

"How do I get them off?"

"There should be another computer screen. Find a way into the system settings and disable the firewalls and security measures. If you can turn those security protocols off you can leave the rest to me."

Alice fiddled with the touch screen, disabling whatever

she could. She was frantic; hardly able to function amid her confusion and her pounding heart.

"Tell me when you're in," she said, continuing to press buttons, now almost randomly. She grew frustrated and hit the screen.

"I'm in," Kyle's voice said through Alice's Bumblebee.

She smiled. She didn't care for computers and was happy that for once, hitting the machine actually made it work. She turned and saw the snake cords detach from Jonathan's head and recoil to somewhere deep inside the machine. She approached the device and put a pale hand on his sweaty and brutalized forehead. She ignored the smell, continuing to admire his sleeping, asymmetrical visage.

"Is he going to be okay?"

"I don't know," Kyle said. "There are a number of factors to consider. His heartbeat could have been synced with the machine, so when the machine shut off, his body would have to adjust to working on its own again. Same with his lungs, really, I just wouldn't know without looking at the machine. It's possible that—"

"WHY ISN'T HE WAKING UP?" Alice screamed at the top of her lungs and collapsed to her hands and knees beside the glorified dentist's chair.

"It's possible his mind is still fighting with itself. Either way, you need to get out of there. Damien and Bain are about to blow that place to high hell!"

≈

*My memories melted off my mind's canvas and pooled at my feet. What was left when the color was gone was not*

# MEMORY LEAK 157

*white or off-white like a painter's canvas. No, it was
black. The kind of canvas one would find in hell. The light
had faded from that place. There was the kind of red tinge
to the darkness you only see if you close your eyes in the
near darkness, examining your eyelids and the blood ves-
sels therein.*

*I was proficient at knowing the differences in light from
behind closed eyes. I spent about a third of my time aware
while Jonathan was asleep or resting his eyes or blinking
and so on. The red tinge of light grew in brightness then
faded back into black. Again and again my eyes flashed
red and then black, until I could tell I was moving. There
were lights overhead. The back of my head regained feeling first. My hair felt like it was being ripped out of my
head. I was surely being dragged. We were being dragged.
I say we, as in, once again of one body and two minds, as
nature intended.*

*I randomly remembered a bit of a poem I had once read
before writings of its nature were no longer considered
useful:*

Who is the third who walks always beside you?
When I count, there are only you and I together
But when I look up ahead the white road
There is always another one walking beside you

*It was unmistakably the work of T.S. Eliot. That man
knew of which wasteland I spoke and of what I see in my
little head. He speaks to me at times more even than Liam
Mail speaks to Jonathan. He knew what it was to feel 'like
a patient etherized upon a table.' I knew at once what it
felt like to be J. Alfred Prufrock.*

*I shuddered at the thought, and Jonathan opened his eyes. I saw a small-framed girl heaving our limp body down the hall from the reeducation room. I told Jonathan he should say something to her. He listened.*

"You're late," Jonathan said woozily.

Alice was startled and dropped Jonathan's legs to the floor. "You were early," she smiled. "Can you walk? I don't think I can drag your ass all the way out of here."

"I'll try," Jonathan said, slowly sitting up and then making his way to his feet, swaying as though he wasn't used to controlling his own body. He looked around the corridor and saw two bodies—Police Units—and a third at the end of the hall by the elevator.

"Is your bumblebee working?"

"I think so. Do you guys hear me?" Jonathan asked.

"Loud and clear, Sleeping Beauty," Mick said. "It worked, the Reeducation Central Nexus is down."

Alice smiled brightly. "Finally…I can't believe it actually worked."

"You made it sound like you had a little more faith in the plan earlier."

Alice averted her gaze, ashamed of herself.

Bain piped up in their ears. "You're still in Symmetry Headquarters? You'll have to use the other exit, this thing is going off in sixty seconds!"

Alice pressed a button on her electronic bangle and pulled up a map of the building. She zoomed in on a small corridor extending from the main structure. "There, let's go."

Jonathan nodded and he put an arm around Alice, leaning on her for support as they plodded along toward the secret corridor. They came to a dead end.

## MEMORY LEAK

"A little help, Kyle."

"Almost there, just hold on," he snapped.

The false wall slid up, closing after they passed through the doorway.

"Keep moving. Knowing Damien and Bain that blast is going to be more than enough to take this place down."

"Can we even make it to a safe distance?"

Alice said nothing, but started walking faster. *I told Jonathan we were screwed. He told me to shut up. I listened this time.* There was a rumbling above them. Dust was already falling from the air ducts and the floor was shaking, growing in intensity all the time.

"Run!" Alice screamed.

*I let Jonathan have every ounce of coordination I could and he ran like he never had before.* Jonathan chanced a glance backward and saw support after support cracking and crumbling and crashing into a pile of dust and debris like dominoes made of C4. They were approaching another wall, another dead end. The rumbling could be felt in Jonathan's chest, *it even made me jump in his skin.*

"KYLE!"

"One more second!"

"NOW!"

The wall slid into the ceiling and as it did, so did three other walls down the hall, revealing more than a hundred meters of clear path to run. They ran and Kyle closed the security doors behind them. The debris crashed through each of them like they weren't there. The sound was deafening—like the heavens themselves were crashing on top of them. At the end of the hall, Jonathan could see a ladder leading up. *Wherever it goes is better than here, I told him.*

Alice ascended the ladder first. While she climbed, Jonathan looked back at the impending destruction, frozen by the sight.

"Jonathan, come on!"

He climbed, quickly catching up with Alice. Kyle closed a metallic hole beneath them, which looked like a chameleon's eye closing. Eight metal pieces spiraled toward the center point and blocked the debris from ascending any further. *At least that was how it was supposed to work. What actually happened? The debris crashed through the metal spiral and one of the shards cut into Jonathan's back before impaling the wall next to him.*

Jonathan cried out in pain. *I took Jonathan's mind to another place, a happy place if you will, and blocked the pain from his mind.* The debris was crushing the vertical tunnel they were ascending and it was gaining on them. *I told him to get moving.* The ladder vibrated under Jonathan's hands. They were approaching what seemed to be the top.

They reached a platform and ran across to an elevator with exposed metal railings. Alice punched a green button on the railing and the platform began to ascend with unexpected speed. The debris reached the top of the ladder and curled around to the miniature elevator shaft, which was only big enough to hold the two of them. At the top of the elevator's track, they stepped out onto the platform. The wall read 'zero.' Alice spotted a final ladder and quickly climbed it. Jonathan followed in her wake, but a circular hatch stopped them from reaching the surface. He lowered his gaze through the holes in the metal grate of a platform below them. Gray dust rose up violently. They might have escaped the debris, but Jonathan heard a second blast, and

# MEMORY LEAK                                    161

now he knew the entire building had collapsed on top of itself. Their side tunnel wouldn't last forever.

"Can you open the hatch, Kyle?" Alice asked frantically.

"It's not in the system, you'll have to do it manually."

Alice turned the wheel of the circular hatch, much like the top of a submarine, and pressed several buttons Jonathan couldn't see, probably at random. *She pressed 03830—which had one line of symmetry. It was possible that Liam Mail had OCD.* Just when Jonathan was losing hope, the hatch made a beeping noise and opened. They were finally at street level. Alice and Jonathan climbed out of the hatch and ran for cover. *I made a mental note to ask her how she came up with the code when all of this was over.*

The ground shook and the concrete split open for a block in each direction. Pieces of metal and dust and earth shot into the air like a geyser that's been held back by some unseen force, the pressure building and building until it finally exploded upwards and downwards and sideways and every way. After the explosion of matter, the concrete depressed into a massive divot, a crater the size of several city buses. The concrete sank beneath their feet as they ran and jumped reaching what would become the edge of the deepest crater Jonathan *or I had* ever seen. *We would later discover that Alice had seen a crater nearly twice as big in her youth, but that is neither here nor there.*

Alice and Jonathan now lay on their stomachs covering their necks and heads with their hands, *not that it would have done much good if the debris had hit them. Luckily for them, they didn't suffer any permanent injuries from the explosion.*

The escape tunnel had deposited them a few blocks away from Symmetry Headquarters in the middle of an empty street. From their position they could see the cloud of smoke above what once was the Symmetrical skyscraper. Damien and Bain had outdone themselves. It was a surgical strike. Each floor had collapsed upon the one below it, two hundred stories in all, leaving the surrounding buildings covered in dust and debris but—as if by some miracle—still standing.

"What was that tunnel just now?"

Alice let out her breath, which she had been holding much of the last stretch of their escape.

"Kerrek's always been paranoid. He had a series of tunnels built from Symmetry Headquarters to other government buildings. Reshape and the Holo Station for starters."

"Where are we now?" Jonathan asked, his eyesight fuzzy from the dust of the explosion.

"Just up the way is the Holo Station. That's where we're headed. Lee and Kingston should already be inside."

"What are we going to do there? I thought our target was the Reeducation machine."

"It was, but we weren't sure if it would actually work. The next phase of the plan was infiltrating the Holo Station. There is business to be done there. The destruction of Symmetry Headquarters has provided us with an opportunity, one we've never had before. By now they are so focused on the Symmetry building their security will be horseshit."

"So I was just the bait after all?"

"No. Because of you we were able to crash the

# MEMORY LEAK 163

Reeducation Central Nexus. If we had just blown up the building it would have only affected this city. Because of you we affected at least the whole region, maybe even more."

*I wasn't convinced, but Jonathan wanted to let it go for now. I agreed, only because I could hear the spinning and chopping of the air above us.* A helicopter descended upon Alice and Jonathan, Kerrek Reinier hanging out the side door with an old-fashioned chrome pistol in hand. The helicopter descended, two hundred feet, one hundred and fifty feet.

"How did he survive?" Alice asked.

"Before they fired up the machine he said he had to take care of something. He must have gotten out before the explosion."

Kerrek fired a few shots, which pinged off the concrete at Alice and Jonathan's feet.

"Forget it, run," she said frantically.

The helicopter had nearly touched down on the cracked concrete when Kerrek jumped out and pursued them on foot. A few Police Units followed behind him, unable to keep up with Kerrek's surprising speed. Alice and Jonathan slipped into a nearby alley and ran through the shadows and the half-light until they were across the street from the Holo Station. Alice took out her energy pistol, fiddled with the settings, and fired at a dumpster in Kerrek's direction. *To Jonathan and my surprise, the dumpster seemed to absorb the energy for a second, then the metal container exploded, shards of metal and remnants of lightning-like energy flying in every direction.*

"That won't buy us much time," Alice said. "We have to move fast."

*Jonathan and I nodded in our collective skin and followed her across the street, to Jonathan's old place of employment, the Holo Station.*

# 22

Kingston scratched his still-fresh dragon tattoo as the elevator smoothly climbed to the top floor of the Holo Station.

Lee regarded him with cold and dark eyes. She gave a soft sigh. "If you keep scratching, it's going to get infected."

"Can't help it," he said, trying to occupy his hands by checking his weapons. "I'm nervous."

"Don't be ridiculous, we've gone up against the symmetricals countless times," Lee reasoned.

"We've never attacked them head on before. We might take them out one or two at a time, but this…"

Lee gave Kingston a look of sympathy for one fleeting moment, then her face hardened once more. "Stay frosty, King. We're almost to the top."

Kingston nodded his big head in response.

"Are you in yet?" Mick asked.
"It's not as easy as you think. I can't just flip a switch

and tap into the city's video feeds. I have to bypass security and keep them from tracking our signal at the same time. We don't want them showing up at our doorstep."

"Yeah, right, don't want that," Mick agreed.

"Until I can hack this, I need you to keep an eye on their bumblebee signals. Alice and Jonathan are almost to the Holo Station but they're being followed," Kyle said and passed Mick an electronic bangle with a city map spread out in three dimensions of red laser-lights. The map was about one foot by one foot

Mick attached the bangle to his wrist, wincing with pain when it tested his DNA, and zoomed in on the image of the city. What once was a one-foot by one-foot image of Nattan became a two-block picture of the area near the Holo Station. He could make out two yellow dots being followed by three blue squares. Mick tapped one of the yellow dots and the image scrolled along with their progress.

"I'm just supposed to watch?" Mick asked.

"If you see any other blue squares following them, we let Alice and Jonathan know their location. About all we can do at this point is watch and keep them informed. That is, until they get to the hundredth floor."

Mick gulped down a wad of spit and watched the yellow dots move quickly toward the Holo Station.

"I think that was the biggest one yet," Bain said, examining the wreckage of the Symmetry building from a rooftop down the street. "How'd you manage to limit the collateral damage?"

# MEMORY LEAK

"Practice. It helps that there are so many sub-floors to the Symmetry building. A lot of the rubble went down and then out the tunnels rather than out at street level."

"Well, Alice and Jonathan got out, so I guess that means we go to phase two," Bain said.

"They should be showing up any time now."

Damien looked over his right shoulder toward the nearest police precinct. Bain leaned over the edge of the roof's railing, following suit.

"Speak of the devil."

Damien lifted a massive gun onto the railing and pointed it toward the approaching Police Unit vehicles. The gun was made of a composite material, which held a blue orb near the end, glowing with the rage of a hundred bolts of lightning itching to be let loose into the night sky.

"Phase four," Damien said with his booming voice and fired the blue orb at the street below. The orb cut into the concrete, then exploded up into a giant arc of electricity and rubble. Everything within a hundred feet of the blast was electrocuted; the Police Unit vehicles shut down, their computers useless. The Police Units retreated from their cars, some of which were now ablaze, and found their visors useless as well. They took off their helmets and let them drop to the cracked concrete below. Bain looked at their faces through the scope of his rifle, his face contorted when he saw them.

"Do you see what I see?" he asked Damien.

"I see it. It's as I thought," Damien sighed, "they really aren't human anymore."

Alice and Jonathan pushed their way past the glass doors leading to the lobby of the Holo Station. Jonathan stopped after a few echoing steps, stunned. Six Police Units lay dead on the floor. Most of them were shot with energy weapons but a couple had less humane incisions and bloody holes from real gunshot wounds. The sight and smell of the blood made Jonathan sick. *His stomach wasn't as strong as mine. I said nothing as he knelt and vomited profusely on the cold marble floor. It wasn't worth the fight.*

Jonathan looked down at one of the men, tempted to look under his visor which continued to scroll information in green letters against the black glass like an old-fashioned computer. *I told him he didn't want to remember what was under their mask.*

"You know what's underneath?" Jonathan asked me under his breath.

*Unfortunately. It's not a sight you ever want to see again. Those eyes—I remember them all too well.*

Jonathan hesitated. *He found my description vague, as he should have, because I was purposely being vague. He can never know what is behind that mask. He would never be the same. And if he were never the same, I would be forced to change in kind.*

After a few moments of staring at the visor with the scrolling green letters and numbers and pictures, Alice called to him and he followed her to the bank of elevators. *I was grateful to her for that. She saved me the trouble of stopping him myself.*

The elevators were made almost entirely of glass, extending out the back end of the Holo Station, in a half-hexagon shape. As one ascended the outer track, they

# MEMORY LEAK 169

could see the entire city beneath them. Alice called an elevator.

A couple of shots were fired and the glass front doors of the Holo Station shattered into tiny symmetrical pebbles on the marble floor. Kerrek stepped through the hole, particles of glass still falling and lodging in his hair, and pointed his pistol in Jonathan's direction.

"It's pointless to run, Jonathan," Kerrek said while approaching the bank of elevators slowly, still a good distance across the lobby.

The elevator gave a bright dinging sound and the doors opened. The two of them stepped inside, where Alice repeatedly hit the close-door button.

"That doesn't help you know," Jonathan said, regretting it as soon as the words left his lips.

Before the doors closed all the way, Kerrek fired a shot through the crack, the bullet lodging half in and half out of the glass, which must have been bulletproof. Alice gave Jonathan an annoyed look and pressed the button for the hundredth floor. The symmetrical half-hexagon rose up high above the city, as if trying to escape the night. Only fluorescent Liam-Mail-approved light bulbs and the laser lights, which flooded the Holo Station, lighted Nattan. Jonathan looked beneath his feet through the smaller half-hexagon of glass and watched the ground get farther and farther away. The elevator seemed sturdy, made of a type of cast iron in the same fashion as the Eiffel Tower. Liam Mail liked the near-symmetry of Gustav Eiffel's masterpiece and looked to France as much as possible when constructing new skyscrapers. *In passing, I mentioned to Jonathan that there was a .34-inch slant on the north side of the structure and a few other minor defects, which barred it from true symmetry. Nevertheless, for the time it was quite a feat of symmetry engineering. Jonathan didn't care about my stream of unconscious ramblings.*

As Jonathan watched the city below, ignoring my comments, he realized for the first time that he wasn't afraid of heights. When he looked at Alice he realized that she did not share his fondness of high places.

"You all right?"

"F-Fine, just don't let go," Alice said, voice wavering and grasping Jonathan's hand with all her might, keeping her feet on the section that wasn't glass.

The circular lights in the elevator told Jonathan they were passing the $20^{th}$ floor. It was at this point that he noticed the elevator music was louder than before. Perhaps it was his imagination, or perhaps Liam Mail was messing with him.

Jonathan heard two faraway pops and cracks, followed by the shattering of glass. Kerrek Reinier was in an adjacent elevator with two Police Units. He had just shot out the glass of his own elevator's wall. *Well, he didn't really shoot it out.* He fired two shots into the glass and then kicked it out with the help of the two Police Units.

*I wondered if he would have the firepower to bust through our elevator's glass. I didn't tell Jonathan what I was thinking, but he had a very similar thought.* Jonathan moved to the outer rim of the elevator, which was made of a thick piece of metal and was more likely to withstand repeated gunshots. Jonathan chanced a glance down at Kerrek's elevator. One of the Police Units was handing him a different weapon.

Kerrek Reinier held this energy weapon with a broad smile across his face, as though he were a kid with a brand

# MEMORY LEAK

171

new toy. He pointed the new weapon at Jonathan's elevator. An orb of blue spun around the tip, raw energy building upon itself seemingly indefinitely. *I told Jonathan my thoughts on the weapon. I told him that if that orb of blue hit, we were toast. Jonathan wasn't an idiot. He already knew he had to do something.*

Jonathan pressed the emergency stop button, the doors opened in between floors. Jonathan started to climb up then noticed Alice was still huddled in the corner of the half-hexagon elevator.

He grabbed her arm, "Come on, I've got you."

She reluctantly let him guide her over the section of glass. Jonathan looked down at Kerrek, who was nearing the same floor as them. Kerrek fired the now raging blue orb. It arced toward the glass elevator with startling speed, crashing into it and forcing Jonathan and Alice to the floor. A split second later, it started. The orb of energy started to come through the glass and metal, inches from Alice. Jonathan grabbed hold of some pipes, which extended vertically between the floors, with one hand and kept Alice's wrist in his free hand.

The orb ate away at the elevator and the track and drove the elevator computer wild, every button lit up, every noise the contraption could make, it made. The elevator music sped up and Jonathan realized that it really was music from before Symmetry; only, it had been slowed down beyond recognition. He didn't recognize the song but heard a female voice singing about beauty being in the eye of the beholder. Jonathan had never heard that expression before.

The blue energy-sphere dissipated, taking with it the solid matter of the bottom third of the elevator. Alice's feet had nowhere to go; she fell.

She fell a few feet before Jonathan's grip could tighten around her wrist. She cried out and gripped his wrist as well, creating a much stronger link. *Now, Jonathan wasn't the strongest man and he had been through a lot, so I can't blame him for what happened next.*

Alice kept gripping Jonathan tightly and managed to get her foot up to where Jonathan's was resting, between floors. She used him as a ladder, climbing up him to the floor above, first holding the floor with her hands, then swinging one foot up, and then the other, rolling onto her back and huffing and puffing. *I wasn't sure if it was her fear of heights or climbing up that took her breath away.* She scooted back to the edge, cringed, and helped Jonathan up to her floor, *which was the $58^{th}$ floor, in case anyone was keeping track.*

*I reminded Jonathan that Kerrek could be there in a matter of seconds.* He didn't argue.

Jonathan stood, let out a great deal of breath, and said, "We've got to get to the hundredth floor. It will all be for nothing if we don't make it."

Alice nodded and stood up. "Can we, um, take the stairs this time?"

Jonathan smiled. For the briefest moment he looked at Alice and did not even think about her symmetry. He wouldn't have suspected for a minute that she was the leader of VERITAS. Maybe that's what made her so dangerous.

The number above Kerrek's elevator was getting closer and closer. 54—55—Jonathan made for the stairs, but Alice stood, feet locked in place as if by some unseen force. She took her pistol out of its holster and cocked it.

# MEMORY LEAK

*I didn't know how many energy blasts she had left.* We hoped she would have enough.

"What are you doing?" Jonathan asked. He could see a tear forming in her eye and smearing her eyeliner.

"I have business with Kerrek Reinier. Use the stairs, and take this," she said, throwing him a small proprietary drive.

"What's this?"

"Just play it. My father made it before he died. This whole thing, it was all his plan."

Jonathan pulled out his pistol and said, "You don't seriously think I'm going to let you confront him alone, do you?"

Alice turned and pointed the pistol at Jonathan. "You will or I'll kill you myself. I told you, I have business with him. Business I have to do alone."

The elevator dinged and there was a pause.

"GO!" Alice yelled hoarsely.

Jonathan, *upon my suggestion*, listened to Alice, opened the door to the stairs and ascended, taking the stairs two and three at a time. As the door shut behind him Jonathan could hear two shots fired. He stopped and closed his eyes, tears forming. He looked at the drive in his hand and knew that whatever happened down there, he also had a job to do. Whatever happened, she was counting on him.

# 23

Jonathan felt tears soak into his nearly destroyed floral shirt as he ascended the stairs higher and higher. He tripped and sprawled out face first on the flat section between floors sixty-four and sixty-five. He wondered if he could or even should go on. He had never felt so tired and beaten and unsure and frightened, all at once, no less. It was a cascade of feeling Liam Mail would never have deemed appropriate for a citizen to feel.

*I told him Alice was a big girl and could take care of herself. She would want her father's message, whatever it was, to get out, even if she didn't make it. I was the cool logic center of his brain in that moment. He was lucky to have my voice of reason with him or he might not have stood up, brushed himself off, and ran up the stairs like his life depended on it.*

Jonathan stopped to catch his breath on the 89th floor. He grasped his knees and heaved. Jonathan said aloud, "If Kerrek killed her back there...he could guess where we were going. He could be...on the hundredth floor...when I get there."

*Let's hope he is, that way you can kill him yourself.*

**MEMORY LEAK** 175

"But that would mean that Alice would be dead."

*I thought for a moment. I didn't care much if she lived or died, but she was important to Jonathan. His conscious mind loved her deeply, and my cold, rational mind still didn't trust her. I told him to have faith in her and that she was strong. I would have choked on my own vomit if I had a real body. Who was I to talk about faith?*

Jonathan weighed his options and chose to go on. After all, it wouldn't do him any good to go back down at this point. He climbed the stairs until he came to the hundredth floor, the great green metal door all that stood between him and the Holo Studio where Liam Mail gave his daily address. Inches away from the studio that broadcast to every street corner, every wall screen, and reflected in every window on street level. There was a keypad, the combination of which Jonathan had never known. Nevertheless he tested the handle. The door creaked open and he entered the dim studio.

The only lights were those of the sound and light boards and the faint glow to the floor of the Holo stage. Jonathan took a few steps forward, his breathing labored, and let the staircase door close behind him. Something was wrong. Maybe it was the door to the staircase that didn't require a security key code to enter, or perhaps it was the multiple bodies littering the floor.

*That's what did it for me.* They were the same as the bodies in the lobby, killed by inhumane weapons; weapons from another time. Near the soundboard lay a much more familiar body. Kingston, his huge body with the new dragon tattoo, lay on his back staring up at nothing in particular, a giant bloody hole in his chest as though someone stabbed him with a thick knife and turned it mercilessly 180 degrees. The result was a perfect bloody circle. King was completely drained. The look on his face was pure surprise. He was truly dead. The pool of blood must have been fresh because it still crept toward Jonathan's feet and he could hear a faint gurgling of blood in the slain man's throat. The smell of iron invaded Jonathan's nostrils and made him gag.

The whole thing was a trap. But, set up by whom? *I suggested Alice was behind it. It was just a thought. Jonathan resisted the idea.* As it turned out, Jonathan was right. *I admit it. I misjudged Alice, and it was one of my few mistakes in an almost perfect record. So, who had sprung the trap? Whoever it was currently held a broad combat knife to Jonathan's throat. To our throat, I suppose.*

On the 58th floor, two bodies lay on the ground, struck fatally with an energy weapon blast. Alice's pistol was hot at the tip, sending up a plume of smoke. The laser weapon was aimed at Kerrek Reinier's heart at point blank range. Another handgun, a 2011 reissue of the Colt M1911, was pointed back at Alice, also at her heart. The reissued weapon was equipped with extra short recoil operation and an expanded magazine. Where the man had procured the weapon, let alone the .45 ACP rounds, was anyone's guess.

"You've got guts, kid, I'll give you that," Kerrek said in his deepest and most frightening voice.

"Kerrek Reinier," Alice began, making her voice as formidable as she could, though it still shook, "You'll pay for my father's death."

MEMORY LEAK 177

Kerrek was taken aback. Then, his face turned from surprise to recognition.

"So you're his brat, huh?" Kerrek said and lowered his weapon slightly. "You may not know this, but your father and I knew each other well. We weren't just opposing sides of a coin. Before the war we were partners. Your father was one of the biggest proponents of Symmetry."

Alice tightened her sweaty grip on her weapon. "You lie. My father hated Symmetry."

"He hated that Reshape couldn't fix him. Which is funny because it was his own fault he looked the way he did."

Alice gave the man a look of confusion and he continued, "Your father let the Reshape doctors try new techniques on him, determined to perfect the Symmetry process. He was obsessed with perfection. Quite admirable, I think. Unfortunately, after so many surgeries, he was left disfigured. They kept trying to fix their mistakes and made the situation worse. That's the way you know him. Ever since you were small he was that way. He couldn't take it and moved both of you to Old Town. Have you ever looked in a mirror? Have you ever noticed how close to symmetrical you are? You were a product of a conception clinic, as per your father's request. If you had regular treatments growing up, you'd still be symmetrical."

Alice nearly dropped her energy weapon. She shook furiously. He was a liar, she thought to herself. He was trying to catch her off guard.

"Even if all of that's true, you killed him. Why?"

"He didn't leave me much choice. At first, Symmetry was just an option, something the public could do if they so chose. Your father thought that asymmetricals were a subclass of human, a reminder of a time when evolution was God. But, your father, with a sense of hubris I've never seen before or since, wanted to become God. That's why he made you. He hated himself for being asymmetrical and didn't want you to suffer the same fate. I've never seen someone hate himself so much.

"Don't get me wrong, he didn't want to kill the asymmetricals, only put them in labor camps. Out of sight, out of mind. That's the concept of Old Town isn't it? We allow you to exist to remind ourselves of our superiority. If you step out of line or wander too far into our town, it's our obligation to send you to the factories. They are jobs that someone has to do, and who better than a subclass of human?"

Throughout his speech, Alice listened with cold realization. Her big hazel eyes shook and tears flowed freely down her cheeks, gathering near her chin and falling to the floor. Could she even kill him now? Kerrek admitted to killing her father, but what if her father was a monster? What would that make Kerrek? She closed her eyes and her eyeliner ran like black tears down her face.

"Put down the gun, Alice. You're so close to Symmetrical, the fix would be easy. It would be over by morning. No one else has to die tonight."

Alice's laser weapon writhed in her sweaty grasp. For the first time in her life she was tempted to acquiesce to the Symmetrical world. Was her father really the monster Kerrek described? Her mind was a storm cloud of gray, thundering in her temples. She felt her neck pulse with the pounding of her heart. She might have even felt the blood streaming through her veins, and in that moment, she felt

**MEMORY LEAK** 179

miniscule and weak, like a mortal thing. Like something fragile and temporary, she stared at her free hand and made a fist as though testing her own power. She relinquished her grip and let her shoulders sink. She felt she had overestimated her capabilities.

Her father's message; what was it really? She had never seen it. Was it a pro-Symmetry rant or a late-in-life change of heart? At the very least, she needed to watch the message before it was broadcast to the whole city, or even the whole country, she was unsure how far Liam Mail's power spanned. That wasn't something that was revealed to anyone below Kerrek Reinier's position.

"I'll take my chances," she said, pulling the trigger of her energy pistol. Time seemed to slow and the look on Kerrek's face burned itself into Alice's subconscious, where it would be forever vivid. His arrogant snarl had turned to shock. It was the first time Kerrek Reinier's face had held that pose.

The pistol clicked. It was empty. That was the problem with energy weapons; unlike recoil pistols, energy weapons didn't notify the user when they were empty. Rather, they simply stopped firing, making no noise but the sound of the trigger being pulled.

Kerrek stood, stunned for a second, clearly expecting to be dead.

Alice seized the opportunity and lunged at him, using the butt of her energy pistol on his forehead. Kerrek fell to one knee, dropping his weapon. To Alice's surprise, he didn't stay there long. He swept her feet out from under her. Her pistol skidded across the floor, out of reach. Kerrek reached for his gun but she kicked it away. He cursed and rolled on top of Alice, pinning her.

"Give up! I can make you perfect," Kerrek said while struggling against her wiry strength.

She broke one of her hands free from his grip and retrieved a small knife from a sheath on her thigh. She stabbed the five-inch blade into the closest thing to her hand, which was his upper leg. He stood up and cried out in pain. Alice searched her body for another weapon. She smiled. She had forgotten all about her eight-inch bowie knife stored sideways against her lower back, though she couldn't understand how since it was so large. She drew it, holding it backward in her hand so the blade was almost a part of her forearm.

Kerrek pulled the knife from his thigh, winced, and faced Alice with an anger that she had known was underneath his cool and collected exterior all along. His thigh trickled blood. The knife must not have hit an artery because the stream was slow.

Kerrek stared at the knife in his hand and said, "This is a little dated of you, isn't it? I would have expected a girl your age to be obsessed with the newest toys."

"I want to watch you die," Alice said in a morbid voice she had never used before and doubted she could ever duplicate.

"Strong words for a dead girl," Kerrek said, before lunging at Alice with a speed she thought was reserved for a much younger man.

Alice lurched her body to the left and Kerrek's blade cut the air with a quick swoosh. A near miss. Kerrek turned his thrust into a sweeping slash meant for her throat. Alice drew up her bowie knife and caught his blade in midair; the blades vibrated and made a loud clinking metallic sound. They struggled against each other's blades, push-

**MEMORY LEAK** 181

ing all of their weight into them, testing each other's strength.

Kerrek's face contorted into something repulsive. He held his knife with one hand, the other holding his own closed fist in an attempt to gain leverage. He strengthened his grip on the knife and loosened his balancing hand, grabbing Alice's knife-wrist. She struggled to keep her balance as he moved in for the kill. Alice spun away, falling to one knee and catching her forearm on the length of Kerrek's penknife in the process.

Blood flowed red, hot, and sticky from her dominant arm. Soon the cut was invisible behind a wall of red. She switched the bowie knife to her left hand. VERITAS had taught her that if you go to a knife fight, inevitably, you would be cut.

She didn't let Kerrek cherish his small victory. Her knife flashed and a gash appeared on his left cheek, long and deep. Drops of red dripped until the stream disappeared down his neck and beneath his shirt. They matched each other's cuts for a while longer, a true victor never clear. Their knives flashed back and forth, both Alice and Kerrek recoiled in pain as they were scored with red. Kerrek's face dripped from several gashes, though he didn't seem to notice, too focused on killing his prey.

A few more deep cuts and Kerrek said, "Enough." He stepped back from Alice and held the deepest gash along his face. "This is pointless. If we keep going, we'll both bleed out."

"For you, that's not the half of it."

A look of comprehension crossed Kerrek's face. Most of his wounds had been on his face. The long and deep cuts were the hardest to cure with Reshape treatments and the hardest to hide from the public. Reshape could cut down on scar tissue, but a hint of white would always remain when the cuts were as deep as his. Kerrek Reinier was asymmetrical. Permanently.

"No. You bitch, you tricked me!"

Alice only smiled, holding the gash on her forearm, applying pressure.

Kerrek wobbled backward, his back crashing against the wall opposite the bay of elevators. The look on his face was pure shock. Alice wondered what was happening in his head. What wheels were turning in there?

"This is the worst punishment I could think to give," Alice said with a maniacal smirk. "The way I see it, you have a few options. You could go work in the factories, or you could retreat to Old Town."

Kerrek couldn't register what was happening. It wasn't clear whether he even heard Alice speak. He looked at the five-inch blade in his hand. By the time Alice realized what was happening, it was too late. She was ten feet away with eyes pried open when Kerrek lifted his knife, jammed it through his upper left ribcage, and took his own life.

Alice had seen people die before. She had seen them keel over with the blast of an energy weapon or caught in an explosion and fried to a crisp, but this…this was personal. She never expected to feel remorse or pain or fear or anything else but satisfaction when Kerrek Reinier died. Somehow, this kill, above all others, was the most real to her.

She kneeled next to him as he gasped for air, taking in what would be his final breaths. Blood welled up in his mouth and he cocked his head slightly, spitting and coughing out the vermilion fluid. He tried to wheeze out whatever words he could to her.

"Alic—your fa—her—mean—th—best. Lia—Mai—tru—monster…"

That was all he said. Alice shook him, trying to pry more information from his cold lips. It was useless. He was gone and all that was left was the smell of iron invading her nostrils. Then, Alice did something she never thought she would do in that situation. She cried. She wept because she was responsible for his death, she wept because she couldn't tell if she was happy or sad or angry or just plain frustrated and confused. Liam Mail the true monster? Did that mean her father was innocent? She laid Kerrek's head down softly on the cold floor and stood, holstering her bloody bowie knife. There was only one way to find out. She had to get to the hundredth floor.

# 24

A small cut formed on Jonathan's neck, nothing serious, only a reminder that he was slave to his captor's will. The wielder of the knife walked him forward to the edge of the Holo stage. A man stepped out of the darkness onto the opposite edge. It was a man Jonathan was familiar with but whom he had never actually met.

Liam Mail smiled the same fake smile he used in his addresses. He wore an expensive black suit and fiddled dutifully with the lapels. The man looked as though he was in his mid-fifties, though his hair was only slightly tinged with gray. He was a hardened man, with the face of a soldier, but made symmetrical with hard work and a lot of time under the knife. He held a black rod, about a foot long, though it looked extendable. Jonathan wondered what purpose it could have.

"Jonathan, a pleasure. It's been so long."

"We've never actually met," Jonathan struggled to say under the weight of the knife.

"Nonsense. You've done well, bringing that to me," he said, pointing to the drive in Jonathan's hand. "I've been looking everywhere for it. Your mission was a success."

# MEMORY LEAK                    185

"My mission?" What the hell was he talking about? *I was as confused as Jonathan.*

"Oh, of course. My apologies. For it to work, to infiltrate VERITAS, you would need to forget who you were, naturally. Bring him here, Lee."

Lee? She retracted her knife and shoved him forward and onto his knees. *What could he mean? What mission? Forget who I was?*

"Bring me that body," Liam Mail instructed Lee, pointing to a Police Unit. "You know why they're called Police Units and not policemen?"

"Political correctness?"

"No," he said, pulling off the man's visor.

*Jonathan and I were at a loss for words. The man's eyes were not what I would call eyes.* They were a mess of circuits and dim flashing lights all around the policeman's clouded eyeballs. He wasn't considered a person any longer, not by any conventional standards. The circuits extended beyond his eyes, almost all the way to his ears on either side and down the bridge of his nose. Where his eyes should have been were blue and brown orbs of light, clouded as though he had cataracts.

"Is he human?"

"Technically, yes. We've made some…enhancements. Reversible, for the most part. In a few years, when he was past his prime, we would have erased his memory, inserted a new and nicer one, and removed his implants. It's all quite painless and they don't know the difference. Obviously, if you can't even remember…"

"I was never one of those things."

"You worked for me. A bodyguard, no less. When I saw your potential I thought you could serve another purpose;

a much greater purpose."

"And Lee?" Jonathan asked, looking around at the dead bodies and shaking off the idea that he could have ever been anyone but himself. "If she works for you, why did she kill all of your guards?"

"A recent recruit. She is so nearly perfect; I'm just going to give her what she wants. I live to serve."

*I told Jonathan what we had to do. Liam Mail wasn't leaving us much choice. Whatever we had been, we weren't anymore. We had become our own person, some-one new. Someone had to stop this madness.*

"Bring me the drive, Jonathan."

"What are you going to do with it?"

"Destroy it, of course. Dr. Renegare went off the deep end in his later years. He wasn't himself. The message can't be broadcast to the public. He spoke only lies. He didn't even follow his own motto in the end: *Live Not On Evil.*"

"Dr. Renegare?"

"You should know his daughter, Alice. Dr. Renegare created Symmetry. He also created you. He tried to defy me by creating a symmetrical man who could not be per-manently reeducated. It seems I won out in that battle."

"You're lying."

"Who are your parents? What are their names?"

"Are you joking? Their names are—" Why couldn't he remember?

Lee slinked beside Liam Mail and used her knife to pick blood and grime from beneath her fingernails. She looked as though she were holding back laughter. Why had she betrayed VERITAS so easily? There was a missing piece to the puzzle. Jonathan didn't have to wait long to find out

# MEMORY LEAK 187

what that missing piece was, because just as that thought crossed his mind, Lee lunged at Liam Mail with her full force behind her blade.

Liam Mail dodged easily and hit her with the black rod. The tip glowed blue and a similar blue glow emanated from Lee's back where he had hit her. Over her back, the blue glow oozed out and it began to eat at her spine like an unstoppable acid. *She screamed the most horrible sound Jonathan or I had ever heard.* All control of her body was lost. She writhed on the ground in no particular direction, flopping like a fish out of water. The blue glow, which was more of a liquid now, seeped through her clothes and disappeared presumably under her skin, attaching to her spine. The glow brightened but only for a second, then faded, along with Lee's struggle. She was dead.

Jonathan was in a state of shock. *I tried to reason that she probably wanted the kill for herself, to prove herself in some way. Maybe she was tempted by Symmetry after all.* Why did she kill Kingston, then? Was he just in the way? What a waste.

"Give me the drive, or you'll suffer the same fate. I don't mind prying it from your dead hands."

Jonathan hesitated, held the drive up in the light so he could examine it. It was the size of a thumbnail, blue, and looked like any other drive he had seen before. He wondered what could be so special about a drive that small. It couldn't have held more than a few terabytes of information anyway.

The elevator dinged and the doors slid open. No one stepped out, but a small gray sphere was thrown from somewhere on the elevator. It arced and bounced toward

Jonathan and Liam Mail. *I recognized it from somewhere, but where exactly, I couldn't say. All I knew was that Jonathan should close his eyes. I used my entire will to get him to do so, and luckily he complied.*

From behind Jonathan's eyelids he could make out a burst of light. It must have been a flash grenade. The room was filled with that blinding light and was then left in darkness, only the small gray sphere glowing like a rogue light bulb on the floor. Jonathan's eyes had been burned with the light, despite his closed eyelids, and he felt disoriented.

Regardless, the flash grenade was the distraction Jonathan needed to retreat from the Holo stage before he was caught in the crossfire. Alice erupted from the elevator firing both from Kerrek's pistol and an energy gun. Liam Mail whipped out a gun from his inside coat pocket, firing like a man with everything to lose.

Jonathan fired his pistol from behind the sound and light boards, wasting most of his shots, but finding Liam Mail's shoulder in his final discharge. Alice's pistol clicked empty and her energy weapon simply stopped firing. She threw them both at Liam Mail. She had no clips left anyway; he dodged the first but the second hit him in the forehead. He staggered off the edge of the Holo stage, dazed and cradling his shoulder. Alice joined Jonathan behind the sound and light boards, using their bulk to protect them from stray bullets. Liam Mail had to be running out of ammo by now.

"We'll take him together, on my count," Alice suggested.

"No," Jonathan said. "You didn't see what he did to Lee. He's got another weapon, something I haven't seen

MEMORY LEAK 189

before. It attaches to the spine, I think it's like an acid, dissolving through anything until it can feed on the nervous system."

"Lovely," Alice said frankly, rethinking her position of an all-out rush.

"I've got an idea, follow my lead."

Jonathan stepped out from behind the sound and light boards, confronting Liam Mail, leader of the symmetrical world, who stood up and, brushing himself off, put pressure on his shoulder wound. It was then that Jonathan felt the collective pain of all his wounds, most of them centered on his face, which was a mess of bruises, cuts, and gore.

As Jonathan approached, Liam Mail took out the black extendable nightstick, which promptly formed a blue orb at the tip. The man, who had at one time looked utterly menacing, now looked like a stray dog with his back up against a wall, ready to do anything to survive. He was even more dangerous now than he was before.

Jonathan reached in his pocket and pulled out a small proprietary drive. Liam's eyes lit up. Jonathan threw it to Liam Mail. With his left arm useless, he dropped his blue-orbed rod to catch the plummeting drive. As soon as the rod hit the ground Jonathan was upon him with more fire than hell itself could hold. They rolled on the floor, exchanging blows like kids fighting in the schoolyard, like any sense of control or measured fighting was gone.

Lights kicked in overhead, bright red laser lights, which rotated around the Holo stage and seemingly trapped

Jonathan and Liam Mail inside like an ancient gladiator arena; only, the audience wasn't in the same room or even the same building. Everything on the Holo stage was being broadcast to every street corner, every shop window, and every True Vision Wall Screen in the city, the region, and only Liam Mail knew where else. Liam seemed not to notice the red lights. Instead, he came at Jonathan with intent to kill.

Jonathan hit him several times in the face, unlocking Liam Mail's jaw and hurting his own hand in the process. He pushed past the pain, *with my help*, and continued pounding him in the face until all hope of symmetry was lost. Unlike Kerrek Reinier, Liam Mail's symmetry was lost in front of an audience, the audience that he himself had created. The asymmetrical supreme leader stumbled backward and fell to a sitting position on the ground. He fumbled around for the rod with the blue orb. He found it, smiling a bloody and somewhat toothless smile up at Jonathan.

Liam Mail stood up with the rod extended, prepared to lunge. Alice jumped on his back, bloodied and cut up as she was, and stabbed him with her eight-inch bowie knife. It struck him straight through the heart, if there had been a heart of which to speak. There was, of course, and he died on that Holo stage, in front of millions or perhaps billions of people. They pried the drive from his hands and inserted it into the universal socket on the soundboard.

Liam Mail's holo image was still being broadcast when Dr. Renegare's hologram appeared on the Holo stage bathed in red light. *What Dr. Renegare said was and will forever be ingrained in my memory, even as the exact words fade from Jonathan's conscious mind. Jonathan's*

# MEMORY LEAK 191

*memory of the event was much more meaningful than the words that were actually spoken, but I remember exactly what he said. This is exactly what was said:*

*I am Dr. Erik Renegare and I invented Symmetry. I thought I was creating a perfect world where there was no suffering. I was wrong. It is impossible to make every person symmetrical, and even if it were possible, it wouldn't be right. When some are made symmetrical and some are not, people are forced into a dominant and subservient class. This is wrong.*

*We should celebrate each other's differences and give no one type of person preference over another. People should choose their own marital partners because they love them, not because they are of another race. These forced matches cannot continue. In a few generations there will be only one color of person. That is wrong.*

*I call for Symmetry to be abolished. I don't believe it is necessary to dismantle Reshape. If a person is unhappy with the way they look and they choose to undergo a procedure to change their appearance, so be it. But, no one should be forced to change the way they look. That is wrong.*

Dr. Renegare went on for another five minutes disowning Symmetry and Liam Mail's Police-State regime. Jonathan and Alice weren't sure if their message was even getting out. Jonathan strode toward the window and looked down one hundred floors to the street below. Red figures, Holo images, littered the streets and shop windows. *Oh yeah, I told him, the message was out.* Moments after the broadcast finished, the streets were filled with Symmetrical people, unable to be reeducated, unhappy in their servitude to a government which had its own interests rather than the people's interests at heart. There would be riots that night. *Riots the size I hadn't anticipated; violence in the streets that would change the very landscape of Nattan.*

For a while after the red Holo emitters had faded, Jonathan leaned up against the soundboard in silence. Alice sat in Bob's roller chair at the next station, calmly wrapping her arm in a piece of her shirt. She was the first to speak.

"Jonathan, I have a confession."

"The mugging," Jonathan said. "In the street, where we first met. That was planned, wasn't it?"

"Yeah," Alice said, ashamed.

"The two men?"

"Damien and Bain."

"Why?"

She hesitated, "I found a notebook with the drive, under a floorboard in my bedroom. There were instructions. I had a picture of you when you were younger, your name, and some other pieces of information. It didn't take long to find you from that. The notes said that your mind was impervious to the long-term effects of reeducation. That your mind could cause a memory leak in the system. That it's what you were…made for."

"Made?"

"Engineered, conceived, it's all the same these days. You have to understand, my father was only trying to destroy Symmetry. I didn't know he was the one who created it in the first place…"

"How was I made? Is he my father, too?"

"No, he stole samples from the Cryo-lab."

# MEMORY LEAK

"What kind of samples?"

"It's not important," Alice said, rising to her feet. "We really should be go—"

Jonathan put a hand on her shoulder and forced her back down to a sitting position. "No, tell me, who were they?"

She looked as though she would cry. She began slowly, "Your mother…was a patient at Greendale Mental Institution a little ways upstate. Scientists," she began and choked back tears, "froze her brain and…and one of her eggs when she died…for research. The file…it didn't say what was wrong with her exactly. The whole thing had mysterious circumstances. What they do know is," Alice faltered. "Oh, God. They do know she had multiple per-sonalities…one of which—"

"It's okay. I can take it," Jonathan said, unsure whether he really could take it.

"One of her personalities, killed almost every guard in the Greendale Institution as well as some of the other patients. They shot her, then took what they could. I'm so sorry," Alice said, choking up.

Jonathan stared past Alice into nothingness. He was the child of a murderer; a crazy murderer. *That explains a few things, he thought, giving* a mental nod to me.

*If I can interject, I've helped you in more ways than you give me credit.*

Jonathan ignored me and thought for a moment about something more pressing to him. "And my father?"

"I don't want to say, it's too…it's too horrible."

"Please," Jonathan said in the least crazy-sounding voice he could muster.

Alice's eyes darted to the corpse of the fallen Liam Mail.

"No," Jonathan said.

"Liam Mail was your father; that's what the file said."

"Impossible," Jonathan said, contorting his asymmetrical face further.

"I don't know, maybe it's a mistake. He couldn't have known about you in any case, could he?"

"That would explain why he kept me so close, in the Holo station and as a bodyguard. It would explain why Kerrek Reinier let his daughter be matched with me, so he could keep an eye on me. My God. My whole life has been a lie."

"Liam Mail must not have known who the mother was."

"Why do you say that?"

"He's had dozens of sons created, but he knew who the mothers were. He had approved them. Though, he didn't approve of the sons. They were killed when they didn't meet his expectations. He would have known that you were not a product of an approved genetic pairing, which means he probably kept you alive out of curiosity."

"How do you know all of this."

"My father's files, he's got entire libraries under Old Town. I've only scratched the surface. It's true that Dr. Renegare was behind your birth, you have to see that."

Jonathan stood up and walked slowly to the elevator. It had only been ten minutes since the message had finished, but he could already hear a revolution in the streets. Symmetry really was dead, because of him and Alice and the rest of VERITAS. Jonathan turned and looked at Alice, who did her best to hold back tears and come across as strong.

"I guess 'live not on evil' depends on your definition of evil," Jonathan said.

# 25

Jonathan stared at the ensuing violence from the safety of the descending half-hexagonal elevator. It wasn't what Jonathan had imagined would happen if Symmetry fell. Every government supplement outlet was being looted, people gathered every tool, every scrap of food, every piece of clothing they could and horded it in their tenements. It was anarchy.

Alice joined him at the window, one hand on her lower abdomen, the other attached to the railing with bone-white knuckles. Jonathan thought it a curious position but he said nothing. She stole a quick glance and stepped away once again, probably frightened by the height. He watched as her look turned from triumph to sadness to disgust, all in one fluid moment. She felt the same as Jonathan. This too, was wrong.

"It's not safe here. I fear it won't be for some time," she said.

"Where will we go?"

"We should regroup first and go from there. Kyle, do you copy?" she spoke to her bumblebee. "To the rendezvous point. Damien, Bain, can you make it there?"

"We're leaving now," Kyle said.

"It's crazy down here," Damien said in a deep and disgusted voice. "We'll have to use the sewers to get there."

"Copy," Alice said. "Jonathan and I are on our way."

"What about Lee and Kingston?" Mick asked.

"They won't be coming," Jonathan said.

Alice seemed to have forgotten about Lee and Kingston. She bit her lip and wrapped her arms around her chest like she was going to be sick. Jonathan put an arm around her and led her toward the bay of glass elevators. Inside the descending glass cage, Alice's eyes remained shut and her face pressed against his chest. He realized how hard it must have been for her to come up the elevator by herself, terrified as she was of heights.

No one was in the lobby when the elevator doors creaked open and Jonathan saw his mirror image split in two once more. No one was in the lobby. No one alive, that is. Multiple bodies were scattered around the marble floor; even more than Jonathan remembered. *I reminded him that there were exactly the same number as before. The conscious mind plays tricks on people. That's why I'm here.*

Jonathan and Alice jogged past the symmetrical bits of shattered glass at the front door of the Holo station and into the mayhem of the crowded street. Alice knelt in the middle of the street; symmetricals ran to and fro, arms full of worthless junk that meant only slightly more than nothing to them. Alice used a stray Police Unit riot baton to pry a manhole cover open. He helped her slide it aside and they descended into the calm of the sewer, escaping the din of the street above, and closed the lid.

They ran through the darkness, only the glow from

MEMORY LEAK

Alice's electronic bangle lighting the way. They were running south, as far as Jonathan could tell, toward his old tenement and Old Town to the south of that. They jogged along for ten minutes, easily covering a mile of underground, though there was no way to be sure. That was when Jonathan and Alice heard voices up ahead. At a four-way junction Damien and Bain stood in wait.

"About time. We were about to go on ahead," Damien's voice echoed through the dark.

"You had a head start," Alice said without emotion.

That's all that was said at that time. The four of them knew what they had just done would change everything, for better or worse; everything that happened from then on was on their shoulders. It was the price they paid for change. Jonathan wondered if there could have been any other way to overthrow Symmetry. There was no simple answer. He put it from his mind, *gave it to me to ponder*, while he ran alongside Alice and Damien and Bain to the south, to Old Town.

After a few minutes, Jonathan stopped; the others continued on for several strides until they noticed his absence. Jonathan stopped because through an overhead grate he could see moonlight, and that moonlight made a small circular object on the wet sewer floor glint, reflecting that lunar representation of the sun back at his eyes. *His brain interpreted the images feeding through his eyes and then it was my job to help him make sense of what he saw.* It was a ring just like the one he had given to Elle. The government, who inscribed it with the words 'Live Not On Evil,' gave the ring to him.

Jonathan picked up the ring and placed it gently on his right ring finger, for safe keeping, he told himself *and therefore he told me.* He joined the others, who said nothing and continued running through the damp and the dark recesses of the city's underworld. While he ran, pushing aside the few rats of the northern sewers, he tried to justify picking up the ring. He calculated how far they had run and the distance from the Holo Station to his tenement. It could very well have been the same ring he gave Elle. Then again, it was the standard ring everyone received when they were matched with another person. Still, Jonathan wanted to believe in fate.

The sewer, which was thick gray brick throughout the new parts of the city, changed to brown stone. The tunnel was older and the amount of rats increased dramatically. Jonathan shuffled his feet, *remembering to do so without any of my help*, and made his way past the bulk of the rodents to D-Site, as they called it. The room was an exact replica of B-Site. The rats didn't seem interested in going inside the sewer-room, perhaps from experience. Jonathan realized that the rats were probably the main food source for most asymmetricals.

They entered the small meeting room; Kyle and Mick were already sitting at opposite ends of the table chattering back and forth. When the team entered they stopped talking and the mood of the room turned serious. Everyone sat except Alice, who paced around biting at her thumbnail with a worried look.

"All right," she said and faced the team. "Despite losing Lee and Kingston, we should view tonight as a step in a direction, though I'm not sure which direction that is yet."

"What happened to Lee and Kingston?" Kyle asked. "Their bumblebees went offline before you entered the Holo Station."

# MEMORY LEAK 199

"From what I could tell," Alice said. "Lee saw an opportunity to take down Liam Mail. Unfortunately, that opportunity involved sacrificing Kingston. It was a foolish move."

"King…" Mick mumbled.

"I can't believe she would be capable of something like that," Kyle said. "She and King went way back."

"Is this what we're coming to? Killing each other to get to the symmetricals?" Mick said.

Damien was noticeably silent. Bain nudged him and nodded toward the group.

"Lee," Damien began, "wanted the glory for herself. I didn't think she was serious when she came to me. She said she thought Alice wouldn't have the guts to carry out the mission, and that killing Liam Mail was our best and only viable option. If I had known Kingston had factored into that plan…I would have stopped her."

Alice broke in. "We can't dwell on what might have been. What matters is where we go from here. The people are scared and they need someone to lead them."

"I vote Alice," Mick said immediately.

"No," Alice said sharply. "No one here should lead us. We're part of the problem. We need an outsider, someone with no connections to Symmetry for better or worse."

"Where will we find someone like that?" Bain asked, running his hands through his white-blond hair.

"I don't know. But that's what my father would have wanted. I vote we dissolve VERITAS for now, go our separate ways, and search for a person who could lead us. My father had a library in an underground room a lot like this one. There are dozens of these sewer-rooms scattered around the city. In the notebook I found, he spoke of a time when everyone's voice mattered. I'm going to find his library. Maybe he had a plan. If I can find that room, maybe I can figure out what we're supposed to do next."

"What do we do about the riots?" Jonathan asked. "Surely they're turning more violent by the second. Who knows what the surface could look like by now."

"We have to assume that Symmetry isn't truly dead," Alice said solemnly. "Someone will take Liam Mail's place and offer peace and safety in exchange for privacy and freedom. Without reeducation they'll have a tough time maintaining control. We have a brief window of opportunity, a year, maybe two, to fix this. We have to tell the people, one at a time if need be, that the time can come again where freedom exists over Symmetry."

The five of us that were sitting rose up and made a silent pact. None of us would stop until this mess was fixed. Damien and Bain left the same way they had come in. Kyle and Mick went out the back door, then split to the left and right respectively. Alice and Jonathan lingered at D-Site a moment longer.

"Do you think we can find someone who can lead us?" Jonathan asked.

"We have to. The Liam Mails of the world will keep popping up when they see an opportunity and enslave us all. I just hope we didn't create the perfect opportunity for another Liam Mail to step up."

"What should I do now?"

"We haven't had any communication beyond the edges of the city since the armistice. Someone has to find out what happened and how far the Police State really goes. Are you up for it?"

*I told Jonathan this was the perfect opportunity to*

# MEMORY LEAK 201

*escape. He could flee to the north and cross the border. He could escape the riots and violence and escape the scheming asymmetricals at the same time. I told him he couldn't trust Alice, because he obviously couldn't. I could tell that he didn't see things the same way as me, though it wouldn't matter in the end, because the paths we wished to take were the same for the time being.*

"I'll head north. I've got a good feeling about north."

# Epilogue

Jonathan had been walking for days, his face wrapped up in a long, dark scarf to allay the wind. Alice was kind enough to lend him enough gear for his journey, wherever it would take him. He was a few miles from the point where the brown haze overtook the highest tower of Nattan. A cloud of dust and spinning particles of earth had replaced the city skyline in the distance. He checked his compass: due north.

The sun was setting in its blood-red fashion to his left, the burning light still filling the cracks of the desolate wasteland at his feet. He remembered his dream; had it been a dream? Perhaps a vision of the future? No, that was crazy. *I told him we had been in that wasteland and under that sun once before, on a mission of indeterminate length and of an indeterminate cause. In truth, I couldn't remember much from my time in the military.*

He caught sight of a purple and blue butterfly. It was the only living thing he had seen in days. From what he could discern, the butterfly's wings had symmetrical patterns. It was symmetry by nature's design. It circled his head a few times and then flew west, chasing the red sun.

## MEMORY LEAK

Jonathan tightened his jacket around us. It was late fall and the cold months were fast approaching. Where forests once stood there were the dead trunks of cracking trees. It was a dead place, a place Jonathan only went to in his nightmares. He wondered what had happened to change the landscape so dramatically. He had left what in retrospect seemed a safe haven compared to this rugged wasteland. He didn't even know where to begin his search. Jonathan checked his compass one last time and caught his reflection in the shining glass. *I reminded him that when the sun finally set, the wasteland would grow much colder.* He thought of what would happen to the butterfly in the stinging cold. Ignoring me, he stood silently, frozen for a moment. He smirked, and then said aloud, "I'm perfect."

CPSIA information can be obtained at www.ICGtesting.com
224206LV00001B/46/P